How NOT to Spend Your Senior Year

**Laugh your way through these other
romantic comedies!**

How NOT to Spend Your Senior Year
BY CAMERON DOKEY

Royally Jacked
BY NIKKI BURNHAM

How I Spent My Last Night on Earth
BY TODD STRASSER

From E to You
BY CHRIS D'LACEY AND LINDA NEWBERY

Ripped at the Seams
BY NANCY KRULIK
(coming soon)

Available from Simon Pulse

How NOT to Spend Your Senior Year

CAMERON DOKEY

17968

Simon Pulse
New York   London   Toronto   Sydney

First Simon Pulse edition January 2004
Copyright © 2004 by Cameron Dokey

SIMON PULSE
An imprint of Simon & Schuster
Children's Publishing Division
1230 Avenue of the Americas
New York, NY 10020

Designed by Ann Sullivan
The text of this book was set in Garamond 3.

Printed in the United States of America
10 9 8 7 6 5 4

Library of Congress Catalog Number 2003111969
ISBN 0-689-86703-4

For Georgiana, Heidi, Maurine,
Susan, and Zan:
The staff of Magnolia's Bookstore—
Best pals any writer could have

How NOT to Spend Your Senior Year

One

The story you are about to read is 100 percent true.

No, honestly.

Of course some things have been changed to protect the innocent. But you'd expect that. It's standard operating procedure when it comes to based-on-true-events stories. If this were a techno-thriller, I could say SOP. And I suppose I could anyway. Parts of my story *are* quite thrilling, though there really isn't anything particularly techno about them. Except for this one part where . . .

Okay. Wait.

I can't believe this is happening.

I'm only a couple of paragraphs into this, and already I'm starting to tell things out of order. A thing which is pretty danged annoying, I must admit, though it does bring up an important question, which is as follows:

Where does my 100-percent-true story truly start?

I suppose you could say the whole thing started the day I was born. I'm thinking that's a bit extreme, though. As an alternative, I'm going to go with the third grade, which I think makes me about eight years old. I'm choosing this because that's the year my mom died, and my dad and I moved for the very first time.

Actually let me rephrase that. This is an important point, and I need to make sure I get it just right.

That's the year my mom was killed in a hit-and-run collision, and my dad and I moved for the very first time.

Way back then, of course, I had no idea that these events were related, or that changing location on the spur of the moment was, paradoxically, about to become one of the most important constants in my life.

Just how often *did* we move? Let me put it this way: To the best of my knowledge, I am the only person in the entire United States to have attended fourteen different elementary schools between the third and sixth grades.

That's 3.5 schools a year, in case you're counting.

The pace slowed down a little bit in junior high to 2.5 schools a year, then settled down to an even two for the years I was in high school. Except for senior year, of course, but I'll be explaining more about that in a moment.

Why did we move so much? You're no doubt also wondering. The answer to this one is pretty simple.

I don't know.

Or, here's more of that getting-it-just-right thing again: I know *now*, but I didn't know at the time. I didn't even ask about it, to be completely honest. By the time I was old enough to question the way we lived, I was so used to the way Dad and I did things that I thought it was normal.

I did stop unpacking my suitcases after a while. This isn't nearly as weird as it sounds. You put your clothes away in dresser drawers. I put mine away in suitcases. In both cases, folding was involved. It also wasn't nearly as depressing as you might think. In fact, you can pretty much stop waiting for me to reveal my inner-trauma girl about this, because I simply haven't got one.

Over the years my dad and I developed a routine when it came to moving. Actually two routines: One for leaving a place, and another for arriving in one. But no matter where we went, the living quarters were always the same: a furnished apartment. This was another aspect of life I simply never thought to question. I think I was about twelve before it finally dawned on me that not all dwelling places came complete with couches.

Regardless of the apartment's location, my father and I always performed the same action upon stepping across the threshold for the very first time. We looked for the perfect location for this big gold-framed photo of my mom. Dad packed it in one of his own suitcases, but he always let me pick out the spot for it. Without fail, I looked for a place that would let me see Mom's picture the moment I walked in the front door.

Not that we were morbid about this or anything. We both knew my mom was gone. But we didn't have to pretend she'd never existed, my dad said. Getting out the photograph was just one way of demonstrating the way she lived on in our hearts.

Our leaving routine was slightly more complex and involved two distinct phases. Phase one involved *Phone Calls of Mysterious Origin*. These always came in late at night and went on for several nights in a row. Though the calls were another thing I got so used to I never questioned my dad directly, I did come up with a couple of theories about them:

a) They came in at night in the hope that I would be asleep and not hear the phone ring.

b) Dad never talked long, so it couldn't be a new girlfriend. Therefore, the caller had to be another guy.

I mean, can we just get real here for a second? I'm a girl. When do I *not* hear the phone?

After a couple of days, the *Phone Calls of Mysterious Origin* would cease as abruptly as they'd started. A day when nothing special seemed to happen would go by. Secretly I'd begin double checking my suitcases, making sure everything was in order, because I knew what was coming next.

That would be phase two. In phase two, *The Map* got involved. The really big one of the whole United States that covered the entire kitchen table when we opened it.

"Hey, Jo-Jo," my dad would call out as he heard me come in the door. Dad does freelance research. Or maybe, considering our lifestyle, the term should be free-range. He spends most of his day sitting in front of his laptop looking things up for people he almost never sees. Not your standard Dad-type job, I must admit, but it did have an advantage for us in that he could work from home no matter where home was.

He calls me Jo-Jo because that's my nickname. My full name is Josephine Claire Calloway O'Connor, if you have to have it all spelled out. Usually I'm just called Jo. Or, occasionally, Jo-Claire, if my dad is seriously annoyed with me about something.

Dad's name is Chase William, a name I've always thought sounds exactly like a relay race. I've never heard anybody call him by either one of his first names. Instead people call him Con. That's short for O'Connor, not a negative character assessment, by the way.

"Guess where we're going," my dad would say, gesturing to *The Map* while I put my backpack on the counter and headed to the fridge for the glass of juice I'd poured before heading out for school that morning. Just another example of being prepared. I probably would have been a Girl Scout if we'd stayed in one place long enough.

"Is it warm and sunny with no big bugs?" I'd inquire. This had been my standard question since I was ten, mostly because I thought it described Southern California. If we had to move, why not close to Disneyland?

"Sunny and warm?" my dad would exclaim, scrunching up his face in mock horror. "Where's your sense of adventure, Jo-Jo?"

"Gee, Dad, I don't know. But if you give me a minute, I'll find it and pack it."

At this, my father would laugh and tousle my hair, a thing which occasionally resulted in juice ending up on the floor.

"Here. We're going right here, sweetheart."

With these words, Dad would point to a spot on *The Map*. He never pointed at anyplace even remotely close to Disneyland, a thing I probably don't need to tell you. Pretty much without fail, my dad would have selected some town that even the people who already lived there had barely even heard of.

Not only that, but for some reason I've never even attempted to explain, my father seemed particularly attracted to towns whose names begin with the letter B.

Which explains how I ended up living in Bemidgi, Minnesota; Bottom, North Carolina; Braintree, Vermont (actually, East Braintree); and Boring, Oregon.

Boring was the last small town we lived in, though. And also the last place beginning with B, now that I think about it. I was about to start high school by then, and the next time my father got *The Map* out, he announced that, for the duration of my high school years, we'd be living in a metropolitan area environment, as this would be better for my overall development.

I have no idea how he came to this conclusion. Let's just say I didn't argue.

After Boring, we moved to Clackamas, which wasn't all that far away but did have one key feature of a metropolitan environment which definitely improved my overall development: shopping malls. It also started with the letter C, which I had to figure meant Dad and I were making some sort of progress, even if I didn't exactly know what kind. That's where I began my freshman year.

I finished it across the Washington border, in a place called Enumclaw. I am not making any of these names up, just so you know. Enumclaw is actually slightly east of Clackamas, in a longitude and latitude sort of way. I think it was right about then that I developed this sudden fear that, having spent most of my childhood moving in a westerly direction, my father was now going to touch base at the Pacific Ocean, then start moving us back the way we'd come.

Before I could get up the courage to ask about this, however, we moved again pretty much straight north, to a place called Issaquah. This did allay my moving-back-east fears, though the thought that we might might be headed for the Canadian border did begin to cross my mind.

The rest of sophomore, all of junior, and the beginning of senior year we spent bouncing from place to place on what people in the greater Seattle metropolitan area call the Eastside, by which they mean the east side of Lake Washington.

Right about the time I was beginning to worry that my father had developed a water phobia, about two thirds of the way through senior year, we got a flurry of *Phone Calls of Mysterious Origin*. As a result, we finally did it. We moved to Seattle. And it's in Seattle that the main events of my story actually take place.

There you have it. My childhood in a nutshell.

Before I get completely up to date,

though, there's a thing you absolutely must know. I don't particularly relish confessing this, but I pretty much have to. If I don't, nothing that happened later will make any sense to you at all.

Now that I think about it, I suppose I could have started my 100-percent-true story right here. On my first day at Beacon High. That's the day I did the very last thing I expected.

I fell head over heels in love.

Two

His name was Alex Crawford.

Actually it still is. Nothing terrible happens to him during the course of my story, though it is both fair and accurate to say he does experience some surprises. A thing which makes two of us, now that I think about it.

Alex himself was my very first surprise.

If things had gone the way they usually did at a new school, chances were good Alex and I would never have met. Or, at the most, we'd have seen each other only across a crowded classroom or passing in the halls. He'd take one look at me, maybe notice I was new, then forget he'd ever seen me at all.

No, I am not dissing myself, nor am I suffering from some undiagnosed self-esteem problem of astronomical proportions. I'm just stating the natural result of my number one approach to fitting in at a new school.

Always blend in. Never stand out from the crowd.

This is actually a lot easier than it sounds. All you have to do is be reasonably pleasant to everyone you meet and resist the impulse to make extreme fashion choices.

It's also more interesting than you might expect. To be an observer. To be, as it were, a crowd of one. In my case, it was also the only practical thing to do. There wasn't very much point in getting noticed or getting attached when I knew that, sooner or later, and usually it was sooner, I'd be moving on.

There is one other advantage of not drawing attention to yourself: It makes it much easier to figure out who the players are.

On my left, the computer geeks and skateboard dudes. To my right, the always-dressed-in-basic-black artistic types. Front and center, the popular crowd. Each school has its own unique variations, of course, but in my experience, students everywhere fall into two main categories: those who want to be noticed, and those who don't.

If you fall into the second category, as I always did, you develop extremely good adaptation skills, enabling you to identify the players at a glance, then blend right in to virtually any situation you encounter. After all the new schools I've had to adjust to over the years, I think I can in all modesty state that I possess camouflage skills that can make any blue mutant you care to name look like a total piker.

They all deserted me the day that I met Alex.

It happened my very first day at Beacon, a thing I think I mentioned before. I was standing across the street from the big brick building that would, in just a few moments, become my brand-new (and I sincerely hoped my last) high school, gazing upward. You're probably thinking I was sizing up the school.

I wasn't.

Instead, the thing that had captured my attention was this big metal column topped by . . . absolutely nothing. It was doing this in the parking lot of what I had to figure was the main supplier of off-campus food: a retro-fifties fast-food joint.

Maybe it's supposed to be some kind of art, I thought as I stared at the column. I was living in the big city now, after all. Public art happened. Not only that, it didn't have to make sense. In fact, having it *not* make sense was probably a requirement.

"They took it down for repairs," a voice beside me suddenly said.

I'm kind of embarrassed to admit this, but the truth is, I jumped about a mile. I'd been so mesmerized by the sight of that column extending upward into space, supporting empty air, that I'd totally lost track of all my soon-to-be-fellow students rushing by me. To this day, I can't quite explain the fascination. But I've promised to tell you the 100 percent truth, which means I've got to include even the parts which make me appear less than impressive.

"Huh?"

Yes, all right, I know. Nowhere even

near the list of incredibly clever replies.

"They took it down for repairs," the voice said again.

"Took it down," I echoed. By this time, I knew I was well on my way to breaking my own blending-in rule, big time. Sounding like a total idiot can generally be considered a foolproof method of getting yourself noticed.

"The car that's usually up there." The guy—it *was* a guy; I'd calmed down enough to realize that—said. I snuck a quick glance at him out of the corner of my eye. First fleeting impression: tall and blond. The kind of muscular-yet-lanky build I might as well just come right out and admit I've always been a sucker for. Faded jeans. Letterman jacket with just about every sport there was represented on it.

Gotcha! I thought. *BMOC. Big Man on Campus.*

This made me feel a little better for a couple of reasons. The first was that it showed my skills hadn't abandoned me completely after all. I could still identify the players pretty much on sight.

The second was that in my vast, though

admittedly from-a-distance, experience of them, BMOCs have short attention spans for anyone less BOC than they are. Disconcerting and intense as it was at the moment, I could nevertheless take comfort in the fact that this guy's unexpected and unnatural interest in me was also unlikely to last very long.

"An old Chevy, I think," he was going on now. "It's supposed to be back soon, though. Not really the same without it, is it?"

He actually sounded genuinely mournful. I was surprised to find myself battling back a quick, involuntary smile. He did seem to be more interesting than your average, run-of-the-mill BMOC. I had to give him that.

Get a grip, O'Connor, I chastised myself. "Absolutely not," I said, giving my head a semi-vigorous nod. *That ought to move him along,* I thought.

You may not be aware of this fact, but agreeing with people is often an excellent way of getting them to forget all about you. After basking in the glow of agreement, most people are then perfectly content to go about their business, remembering only the fact that someone agreed and allowing the identity of the person who did the actual agreeing to fade into the background.

This technique almost always works. In fact, I'd never known it not to.

There was a moment of silence. A silence in which I could feel the BMOC's eyes upon me. I kept my own eyes fixed on the top of the carless column. But the longer the silence went on, the more strained it became. At least it did on my side. This guy was simply not abiding by the rules. He was supposed to have basked and moved on by now.

"You don't have the faintest idea what I'm talking about, do you?" he said at last.

I laughed before I quite realized what I'd done.

"Not a clue," I said, turning to give him my full attention for the very first time, an action I could tell right away spelled trouble. *You just had to do it, didn't you?* I thought. He was even better looking when I took a better look.

He flashed me a smile, and I felt my pulse kick up several notches. My brain knew perfectly well that that smile had *not* been invented just for me. My suddenly-beating-way-too-fast heart wasn't paying all that much attention to my brain, though.

"You must be new, then," he commented. "I'd remember you if we'd met before."

All of a sudden, his face went totally blank.

"I cannot believe I just said that," he said. "That is easily the world's oldest line."

"If it isn't, it's the cheesiest," I said.

He winced. "I'd ask you to let me make it up to you, but I'm thinking that would make things even worse."

"You'd be thinking right."

This time he was the one who laughed, the sound open and easy, as if he was genuinely enjoying the joke on himself. In retrospect I think it was that laugh that did it. That finished the job his smile had started. You just didn't find all that many guys, all that many people, who were truly willing to laugh at themselves.

"I'm Alex Crawford," he said.

"Jo," I said. "Jo O'Connor."

At this Alex actually stuck out his hand. His eyes, which I probably don't need to tell you were this pretty much impossible shade of blue, focused directly on my face.

"Pleased to meet you, Jo O'Connor."

I watched my hand move forward to meet his, as if it belonged to a stranger and was moving in slow motion. At that exact moment, an image of the robot from the movie *Lost in Space* flashed through my mind. Arms waving frantically in the air, screaming, *"Danger! Danger!"* at the top of its inhuman lungs.

My hand kept moving anyhow.

Our fingers connected. I felt the way Alex's wrapped around mine, then tightened. Felt the way that simple action caused a flush to spread across my cheeks and a tingle to start in the palm of my hand and slowly begin to work its way up my arm. To this day, I'd swear I heard him suck in a breath, saw his impossibly blue eyes widen. As if, at the exact same moment I looked up at him, he'd discovered something as completely unexpected as I had, gazing down.

He released me. I stuck my hand behind my back.

"Pleased to meet you, Jo O'Connor," he said again. Not quite the way he had the first time. "Welcome to Beacon High. So, where are you from, if you aren't from around here?"

"Pretty much all over," I said, retaining just enough presence of mind to give my standard, non-specific reply.

"O-kaay," Alex said, drawing out the second syllable as if trying to decide whether or not to ask more.

From across the street at the school, the warning bell that signaled the imminent commencement of classes trilled sharply.

"Sounds like we'd better get going," Alex said.

"Uh-huh," I responded.

He stepped back and made a gesture as if ushering me forward. I walked beside him toward my newest school, trying to convince myself that the reason I suddenly felt so dizzy and lightheaded was that I'd contracted some bizarre Seattle flu bug.

Three

You know that phrase, everywhere you go, there you are? Well, my first day at Beacon provided me with the inspiration for a variation:

Everywhere I went, there was Alex Crawford.

Following our surprising encounter in the carless-column parking lot, I'd done my best to return to my normal blending-in behavior, an endeavor which was aided by the fact that first period English was a class Alex and I did not have in common.

I'd timed my arrival at the first classroom with my usual attention to detail. I wanted the room full, but not too full.

Then I'd entered calmly and taken a seat about three quarters of the way back.

This is the seating chart equivalent of the no-extreme-fashion-choices concept, just so you know. All the way at the back says *troublemaker* to the teachers. Too far forward and your fellow classmates think *teacher's pet*.

The inevitable announcement that there was a new student brought the equally inevitable several minutes of unwanted attention. After which, when I did nothing further of note, my new classmates were content to relegate me to the same category as white noise. A thing that was perfectly fine with me. By the time first period was over, my head felt back to normal, and I was well on my way to congratulating myself on my quick recovery from my encounter with Alex Crawford.

Right up until the moment I walked out of the classroom and straight into his arms.

It was hard not to. He was standing right outside the door.

His hands came up to grasp and steady me at the same time as he flashed me that mind-numbing smile. *How on earth did he get here so fast?* I wondered.

"Hey, Jo O'Connor," he said.

"Hey, yourself," I mumbled.

At that moment, I made a snap decision, a thing I usually avoid. My usual new school adjustment techniques just didn't seem to be getting me anywhere, at least not with Alex Crawford. If at first you don't succeed, try try again. Only a fool tries the same thing twice, though. If fading into the background wasn't going to work, maybe standing out by being obnoxious would.

"What did you say your name was, again?" I asked.

Alex laughed. *Oh, nice move, O'Connor,* I thought. It was the same kind of laugh he'd given before. Open, easy, unselfconscious. A laugh that softened all my defenses and pretty much made my heart want to melt like one of those little pats of butter you get at Denny's, left out in the sun.

It also got the attention of anyone nearby who had somehow miraculously failed to notice the extra attention Mr.

BMOC was paying to the new girl. Assuming there had actually been anyone.

"Not to be rude or anything," I said as I took a step back. This forced Alex to let go of my arms. Unfortunately it also resulted in me stomping on the feet of whoever was trying to get out behind me.

"Hey, watch it," I heard him say.

"But I believe it's traditional to let the first-period students exit the classroom before the second-period ones go in," I went on.

"I'm not going in," Alex said simply. "I'm walking you to your next class. History, right?"

Right, I thought. Right before I thought, *This has absolutely got to stop.* If I couldn't nip whatever was happening with Alex Crawford in the bud, there was no telling where I'd end up, though it seemed a pretty safe bet that making a fool of myself would somehow be involved.

"How do you even know where it is?" I asked, my tone aggressive. "What if it's nowhere near where you have to be?"

At this, the student behind me decided he'd waited long enough. He gave a quick shove. An action that sent me right back into Alex Crawford's arms.

"It doesn't make a difference," Alex said.

My brain struggled for most of the rest of the day, but even then, I think it knew that my heart had won.

"You'll like Drama," Alex promised a couple of hours later. We were walking across a wide swath of green lawn that separated the school's Little Theater from the main classroom building. "Mr. Barnes, the teacher, is great. He makes the whole thing really interesting and fun. Even the performing part isn't too humiliating."

"Gee, that's a relief."

On the far side of Alex, I heard a snort of amusement and knew it had come from the third member of our group, a girl named Elaine Golden.

I wasn't quite sure what to make of Elaine. She'd shown up with Alex a couple of times as he'd walked me from one class to another. I had to figure either Alex had asked her to do this, hoping we'd become friends, or she'd tagged along of her own free will, determined to keep an eye on him. It was obvious they were tight, though equally obvious that they weren't a couple. The vibe between them just wasn't quite right.

If ever there was a person whose name suited her perfectly, it was Elaine. Everything about her was sort of . . . golden. She was tall, with hazel eyes and a head of softly waving gold-blonde hair. Even her skin looked vaguely tan, at a time of year when practically everybody else in Seattle still looked like the inside of a mushroom.

"Actually, Alex is correct," Elaine said now. "Even if he expressed himself in a completely pathetic way."

Alex made a face at her. "I get no respect," he sighed.

"Who ran your incredibly successful election campaign?" Elaine asked sweetly.

"Who ran unopposed?" Alex inquired.

"Oh, that," Elaine said.

One of the things I'd discovered during the course of the day was just how big a BMOC Alex Crawford truly was. He'd been class president every year since he'd been a freshman. As a senior, he was considered such a shoe-in for student body president that he'd run unopposed. After graduation, he was expected to follow in his father's footsteps and study law at Harvard, or so a girl with the unbelievable-yet-apparently-true name of Khandi Kayne had informed me at morning break.

This was right before she further informed me she was taking Alex to the girl-ask-boy dance that Friday night. A thing which went a long way toward explaining why my strong instinct had been not to turn my back on her.

"Just so long as you've finished the unit on Shakespeare," I said as Elaine, Alex, and I neared the theater door. We'd go in through the lobby, Alex had explained, but class was actually held in the auditorium.

"I had an English teacher my sophomore year who used to make us read it aloud in class. I was completely hopeless. My tongue kept getting all tangled up."

"In that case, I really hate to break this to you. . . ." Elaine began.

I stopped short. "Please tell me that you're joking."

"I'm joking," Elaine said obligingly. "Unfortunately for you, I'm also lying."

Fabulous, I thought, just as Alex opened the Little Theater door and ushered us through it with a definitely Shakespearean bow.

My first Drama class at Beacon was either:

a) not so bad, or

b) worse than I could possibly have imagined.

Depending entirely on which portion of the period we're talking about.

It started off just fine. The class *was* doing scenes from Shakespeare, a thing you've probably already gathered by now. The bad news was that Mr. Barnes made it clear from the outset that, since I was now a class member, I'd be expected to participate right along with everyone else. Beginning now.

The good news was that the class was working "on book," a term that means with scripts in hand. This meant I wouldn't automatically be at a handicap because I didn't already have something memorized.

I could see right away why Alex and

Elaine liked Mr. Barnes. He wasn't stuffy or pretentious, though he did dress sort of preppy, like he'd originally come from the east coast.

But his whole approach was simple and straightforward. What did the words mean? Why should we care about them in the first place? Why give a rip about Shakespeare after all this time? That complicated high-flown language couldn't possibly be expressing things we'd understand, maybe even go through, could it?

As far as Mr. Barnes was concerned, the answer was, "Duh."

To illustrate his point, Mr. Barnes had chosen scenes from a variety of Shakespeare's plays, all with the same thought in mind: to demonstrate that the emotional content was current, even if the language wasn't. *Romeo and Juliet* was a particularly good example of this. I assume I don't have to explain why.

During the course of the period, I'd watched students enact conflicts between best friends and bitter enemies. I'd heard Romeo talk about his latest girlfriend, knowing perfectly well he was going to forget all about her a few scenes later when Juliet came along.

I'd even read Juliet's lines myself, in a confrontation with her father, and gotten so carried away with trying to make the guy playing Dear Old Dad see my side of things that I'd forgotten all about my previous bout of getting tongue tied.

After each scene, Mr. Barnes prompted the class discussion. What seemed real to us? What didn't? If we suddenly found ourselves in a similar situation, how might we respond?

Then Alex and Elaine got up. They were to be Romeo and Juliet themselves. Not in the famous balcony scene, but the much shorter scene where they first see one another, literally across a crowded room. A crowded dance floor, to be precise.

Alex faced the class, while Elaine stood with her back to us, her face turned in profile. Romeo/Alex then gave his first impressions of Juliet/Elaine.

"O! She doth teach the torches to burn bright. It seems she hangs upon the cheek of night like a rich jewel in an Ethiop's ear; Beauty too rich for use, for earth too dear!

So shows a showy dove trooping with crows as yonder lady o'er fellows shows. The measure done, I'll watch her place of stand and, touching hers, make blessed my rude hand.

"Did my heart love till now? Forswear it, sight! For I ne'er saw true beauty till this night."

Then, as if the measure, the dance that Juliet was engaged in during this speech, had ended, Alex moved to Elaine and Romeo began to act on the strength of his first impressions.

One thing you can definitely say about Romeo: That boy did not waste time. The first meeting between Romeo and Juliet is actually incredibly short. But, before it's over, Romeo has managed to get in two kisses.

Actually, Alex-as-Romeo only managed one.

You could have heard a pin drop—the auditorium was so quiet as Alex and Elaine came to the crucial moment. Slowly, as if testing both her nerve and his, Romeo/Alex leaned in. Juliet/Elaine stayed perfectly still. Softly, almost tentatively, their lips touched.

I wonder what she's feeling, I thought as I felt my own lips begin to tingle. I think that was the moment I acknowledged the truth. I had fallen, hopelessly, for Alex Crawford.

Romeo/Alex eased back from the kiss. He and Juliet/Elaine stared at one another. The air seemed to hum with a funny sort of tension.

These guys are really good, I thought. Then Juliet/Elaine broke the spell. In the scene, instead of melting at Romeo's feet, Juliet makes a snappy, teasing comeback. Maybe Mr. Barnes was right about this Shakespeare-is-relevant thing after all. Not to be deterred, Romeo tries for kiss number two. Elaine waited until Alex's lips were a breath away before providing a snappy comeback all her own.

"I don't think so, pal."

Alex jerked back with a strangled laugh, just as the rest of the class joined in. The two sat down to a round of raucous applause.

"So, what do you think?" Mr. Barnes asked when the class had quieted. "Is what Romeo and Juliet experience love at first sight? Is true love possible after only a few moments, or should we just write off what these two teenagers experience to raging hormones?"

"Is there a difference?" a guy named Matt Kelly quipped.

"In the case of some people, probably not," Mr. Barnes responded calmly.

"Does it *make* a difference?" I heard a voice say over the laughter that followed. "I mean, is whether or not love at first sight is possible even Shakespeare's point?"

"Okay," Mr. Barnes said at once. "What is the point, Jo?" *Now you've done it, O'Connor,* I thought as I realized the voice had been mine. I'd gotten so carried away with my own inner-monologue, I'd spoken my thoughts aloud.

"The point is that *they* believe in love at first sight," I said, somewhat haltingly as every eye in the class turned toward me. "Romeo and Juliet *believe* that they're in love. They believe it so much they're willing to die to prove it. I'm thinking that's a bit extreme, even for hormones."

A ripple of quiet, appreciative laughter traveled through the room.

"And what about you?" inquired Mr. Barnes.

"What about me what?" I asked. "My hormones are fine, so far as I know."

"Thank you for sharing," Mr. Barnes said over another round of laughter. "What I'm asking is: Do you believe in love at first sight?"

I opened my mouth to say of course I didn't. To say that just because I could believe in Romeo and Juliet's love at first sight didn't mean I had to believe in my own.

That was the minute that Alex Crawford turned his head. Just as they'd done first thing that morning, his blue eyes met mine. Alex's eyes were almost expressionless. There was no challenge in them. Instead they seemed incredibly patient, as if they were waiting for something. Looking into them I found I couldn't do the thing my brain was urging. I simply could not bring myself to lie.

"Yes, as a matter of fact, I do," I said.

Then, much to my relief, the bell rang before I could say any more.

Four

The rest of the day passed in a blur, with me trying to recover from what I had done. Instead of blending in as usual, I'd fallen in love. Not only that, I'd as good as admitted it in public.

The day had not gone as planned. At all. A thing which resulted in it being the case that, for the very first time in my entire life, I was actually happy when P.E. rolled around. Not only was it the last class of the day, it was the one place I could be absolutely certain Alex wouldn't try to tag along. Not only that, the class was doing a unit on track and field events.

For reasons I assume I do not have to

explain, running was sounding like a pretty good option.

The only potential drawback was that I shared the class with both Khandi Kayne and Elaine Golden. For obvious reasons, I decided to stick close to Elaine.

"For crying out loud," she gasped now as she tumbled to the grass at the side of the track. "Whatever you're trying to prove, you win. I give up."

We'd been running for a solid forty-five minutes. Not all that long, of course, if you're a marathoner. But I'd have to be the first to admit I'd set a pretty brutal pace. It had taken all of the time Elaine and I had been able to keep going for me to figure out that, no matter how fast I went, I wasn't going to be able to outrun myself.

"I never asked you to pace me," I said as I flopped down beside her, breathing hard.

Elaine sopped sweat from her face with the hem of her T-shirt, propped herself up on one elbow, and glared at me.

"I'm trying to be friendly here, New Girl, in case you hadn't noticed. What is your problem?"

I'm not entirely certain what happened

then. I think it was some variation of *Nothing Left to Lose Syndrome*. Absolutely nothing that day had gone the way I'd thought it would. How much worse could things get if I simply admitted the truth? Especially since it was incredibly obvious.

"I can tell you in two words," I said. "Alex Crawford."

Elaine stared for a moment, an expression I couldn't quite read on her face, then dropped down flat on her back. "You're insane, you know that, don't you? Any girl on this campus would love to have your problem."

"Including you?" I asked, images of the scene from Romeo and Juliet dancing through my mind.

"And come between him and Khandi Kayne?" Elaine answered promptly, her tone sarcastic. "I don't think so. Personally, I'd like to live to attend my own graduation."

"So I was right."

"About what?"

"I thought she spent most of lunch period trying to figure out how to stab me in the back with her plastic salad fork."

Elaine gave a sputter of laughter. "You

know she's taking him to the dance this Friday night, don't you?"

"Of course I do," I said. "She told me so herself. Apparently she thinks this means he'll ask her to the prom."

"Traditional, but not foolproof," Elaine informed me.

"I have a question," I said.

"What?"

"Do you think her dress will have red-and-white stripes?"

"God, I hope so."

There was a beat of silence. Then, at precisely the same moment, Elaine and I turned our heads to look at one another. I'm not sure who laughed first. The next thing I knew, both of us were roaring.

"My stomach hurts," I said when I could speak again. I pushed myself up to sit crosslegged, and Elaine followed suit. "I'm sure it's all your fault."

"Is not," Elaine said promptly.

I could feel the laughter begin to well up once more. "Don't," I said. "If you do, I'll have to hurt you."

"You mean you'll have to try," she said. But she turned her head to look at me, her hazel eyes thoughtful. "You know, I've been trying all day to figure out whether or not I liked you. Or even if I wanted to."

"Gee," I said. "Now there's a surprise."

Elaine smiled slowly, but her eyes stayed serious. "I've known Alex for years, but I've never seen him completely lose his head over anyone."

"For the record, it's not exactly in character for me either," I said, matching her serious tone. "Though I realize you've only got my word for it."

Elaine continued to regard me for a moment. "I think I believe you, New Girl," she said.

"Will you please knock that off?" I inquired. "I have a name. If we're going to be friends, you might learn to use it."

"Are we going to be friends?" Elaine Golden asked quietly.

"I hope we are," I answered, meeting her gaze steadily. "Don't let it go to your head or anything, though. It's just that, with Khandi Kayne around, I figure I could use one."

Elaine's smile spread slowly. This time it reached her eyes.

"It's always nice to be needed," she said.

"Ms. O'Connor, Ms. Golden, the name of this class of Physical Education, not Study Hall. I don't want to have to remind you again."

The voice of the teacher, Ms. Nelson, barked from behind us. Guiltily, Elaine and I scrambled to our feet. At that moment, the bell rang. I had done it. I had survived my very first day at Beacon High.

"Okay, girls! Shower up!" Ms. Nelson shouted.

I grinned at Elaine as we started toward the locker room. "Is that what they call being saved by the bell?"

Elaine nodded. "You know it. And speaking of being saved, how about if I protect you from Khandi Kayne by walking you home?"

"What about Alex?" I asked.

Elaine shrugged. "He has to practice some team sport. I can never remember which one."

I felt some emotion move through me then. Relief or disappointment, I honestly couldn't tell.

"Okay," I said. "You're on."

★

"This is a nice neighborhood, isn't it?" I remarked several moments later as Elaine and I walked along. I suppose, for someone who's spent their whole life living on streets containing houses with lawns in front of them it might not seem so special. It was a new experience for me, though.

Now that I think about it, I should have expected that my first day at Beacon High School would be out of the ordinary. Seattle had already changed an aspect of life that had been the same for as long as I could remember. We were living in a house instead of an apartment.

Furnished, of course.

It was big, two stories plus an attic and a basement. A bank of front windows faced the street, staring out over a wide front porch. There were hooks for a hammock at one end. I could already imagine myself swinging in it, lazing away a summer day.

"Oh, wow," Elaine exclaimed as we headed up the front walk. "Now I know who you are. You're the people who moved into Old Mrs. Calloway's house."

A remark which prompted me to trip

on the steps and sit down abruptly on the porch.

"Walk much?" Elaine asked.

"What did you just say?" I inquired. "I mean, who did you say used to live here?"

"Old Mrs. Calloway," Elaine repeated obligingly as she moved to sit beside me, apparently having decided to cut me some slack over the tripping moment. "Though, actually, I have no idea how old she really was. That's just what all the neighborhood kids always called her. She was kind of a recluse. Never went out much. I think she even had her groceries delivered. She gave out great treats on Halloween, though."

She cocked her head and looked at me consideringly. "Didn't you know her? When you guys moved in right after she died, I thought you must be related or something."

"Not that I know of," I said, my mind doing its best imitation of a hamster on a treadmill. Perhaps I should just remind you why.

Calloway is a part of my name. Josephine Claire *Calloway* O'Connor. And the thing that's significant about that was that Calloway had been my mother's maiden name. Her own last name before she'd married my father.

"I hear it's really cool inside," Elaine went on. "All the neighborhood kids used to dare each other to try and sneak in. I don't know anyone who actually did it, though."

"It is pretty great," I said. "My bedroom has a windowseat. And the bed has this old pink chenille bedspread on it. Our first day here, I fell asleep on top of it and ended up with this weird pattern all over my face."

"Sounds nice," Elaine said.

"I'd ask you to come in," I went on in a rush, "but it's kind of messy since we're still unpacking and stuff."

"That's okay," Elaine said. "I understand."

A thing that made me feel like a jerk, as I'd just told her an outright lie. I never had any boxes to unpack. My belongings were in my suitcases, just like always.

Friends do not lie to friends, particularly brand-new ones. For the record, this is a thing I know. But, sitting beside Elaine on Old Mrs. Calloway's front porch, I also knew I'd had enough. Enough surprises for one day.

Before I could invite Elaine inside my first house ever, there was something I had to do. Something I didn't think she'd understand, as I wasn't entirely sure I did myself. Something important.

"Maybe later in the week," I temporized. "Hey, how about Friday night? We can get all girly and have a sleepover while Alex and Khandi are at the dance."

"What makes you think I'm not going?" Elaine inquired blandly.

I dropped my head down into my hands. The day seemed incredibly long all of a sudden.

"I'm sorry. I didn't think," I said. "Are you?"

"No," Elaine said. "I just didn't want you to make any assumptions."

I gave a strangled laugh. "If ever there was a day to put a stop to that activity, this has been it. Trust me."

"Okay, then," Elaine said as she stood up abruptly. "I guess I'll see you tomorrow." She clomped down the porch steps and moved off down the front walk. "Bet you a latte Alex calls you tonight," she called over her shoulder.

"In your dreams," I said as I scrambled to my feet. "I never gave him my phone number."

"A grande," Elaine specified. She turned back as she reached the sidewalk. "Be ready to pay up, New Girl," she said. "Oh, and by the way, my house is that one there."

She pointed to the house next door.

Shaking my head, I turned around, dug out my keys, and unlocked the front door. As I stepped inside, my eyes automatically performed the first action they always do, a thing they've been doing for so long they now do it completely on autopilot.

They searched for and found the photograph of my mom.

I think I've already mentioned that the first thing Dad and I do when we move to a new place is to find the perfect location for Mom's photo. Out of all the places Dad and I had ever lived, Old Mrs. Calloway's house had the very best spot for it: on the wall right above the center of the mantel.

Other pictures on the wall were undisturbed, but there had been a space in the very center, as if one thing had been taken down. A thing that had been up for a very long time. Its removal had left the wallpaper underneath a different color. Newer, fresher, brighter. There was a faint outline on the wall. An outline that exactly matched the contours of my mom's picture.

"Hi, Mom," I said softly as I crossed the living room to stand in front of her picture. I look a lot like my mother, though I do have my dad's brown hair and eyes. But the shape of my face, the way I smile, all you have to do is look at her photograph to know where those things came from.

Was it just a coincidence that the very first house we'd ever lived in belonged to a woman with mom's last name? Somehow, I couldn't bring myself to think so.

"I'm home," I whispered. "But I bet you already knew that, didn't you?"

Five

That was the moment I secretly changed my name.

To Josephine D. O'Connor.

You're familiar with D, fourth letter of the alphabet.

In this case, it stands for Denial.

Because, as I stood there, staring up at my mother's photograph, I suddenly realized how I was going to handle the fact that I'd just discovered I was living in Old Mrs. Calloway's house.

By doing absolutely nothing.

I suppose you think this makes me a great big wimp, and, under other circumstances, I'd have to admit you might be right. But as I continued to stand there, I swear I began to hear Old Mrs. Calloway's house whispering all around me.

"Unpack your suitcases," it seemed to say. *"You got it right. This* is *your home now, Jo O'Connor."*

"Old habits are hard to break," I said right back. "Besides, for all I know, you won't last any longer than any of the others."

I thought I heard the house laugh then.

"We'll just see about that, won't we?"

"Darn straight, we will," I said. If there was one thing I wasn't, it was a pushover.

"Who are you talking to, Jo-Jo?" my dad's voice suddenly asked.

I jumped and spun toward him. I'd become so engrossed in my dialogue with the house that I'd failed to hear my father coming in the front door.

"Myself," I said. "No one."

"Make up your mind," my father said with a grin as he tossed his laptop case on the nearest couch and came to give my hair a quick tousle. "Hey, I got the scoop on where we should get our pizza tonight," he continued as he moved on toward the kitchen. "There's a place right in the neighborhood that delivers."

I heard several drawers being opened and slammed shut. "Do you remember where the phonebook is?" my father called out.

"That would be in the drawer right by the phone, Dad," I called back. "What's the matter? Photographic memory out of order?"

My dad really does have a photographic memory, by the way. I've always been sort of bummed that I didn't inherit it. I'm thinking it would be a really great attribute on pop quiz days.

The sounds of rummaging ceased as my father stuck his head out the kitchen door. "Don't be a smart aleck, Josephine, or I'll have them put anchovies on your half. You want the usual?"

I grinned. "You bet. And a root beer, don't forget."

"Have I ever?" asked my father.

Having pizza on my first day of school has been a tradition since our very first move. Originally I think my father did it in self-defense. When I was younger, pizza was the one food I could always be counted upon to eat no matter how recently we'd had it, and an extra large would feed us for several days.

We always get a combo, everything on it but the kitchen sink. Then Dad adds anchovies to his half. Gross, but then there's no accounting for grown-ups.

"I'm going to get a salad, too," my father said.

"You're not going to get all health food on me, are you?" I asked as I joined him in the kitchen.

My father never got a chance to answer. At exactly that moment, the telephone rang.

I could feel the color drain from my face. Dad's went completely blank. I saw his eyes widen.

No, I thought as my heart began to pound in hard, fast strokes. *No, it's too soon. Not now. Not yet.*

"You'd better answer it," I said.

My father started as if I'd poked him with a pin.

"Yes, okay," he said. He lifted the receiver and the shrill ringing ceased. "Hello?"

I held my breath.

My father listened, a strange expression coming into his face. Just for an instant, he closed his eyes. When he opened them again, they were dancing with laughter, and something that looked an awful lot like relief.

"Just a moment, please," Dad said. Then he held out the receiver toward me.

"It's for you, Jo-Jo."

"Jo, it's Alex," the voice on the other end of the phone said. "You know—Alex Crawford?"

I took a breath, determined to come up with a snappy reply. Unfortunately for the success of this plan, my mind went blank at precisely that moment.

"Yes, I know," I said. "Hi."

"Hi," Alex echoed. There was a pause that probably only lasted about five seconds but felt like about five hours. "So, you're probably wondering why I called."

"The thought had crossed my mind."

"The thing is," Alex said, "there's this dance Friday night. It's girl-ask-boy. Maybe you heard about it during the day today?"

"Maybe I did," I said. I could feel my

father, hovering just on the far side of the kitchen door.

"So, the thing is . . ." Alex said again. *He's nervous,* I thought. This probably reveals something incredibly dysfunctional in my psyche, but all of a sudden, I felt much better. The Big Man on Campus was nervous about calling me, New Girl Jo O'Connor.

"I'm going," Alex said.

"That's nice," I replied. I heard him expel a breath into the phone. I thought he was laughing, but I couldn't quite be sure.

"I don't want there to be any misunderstanding," Alex plowed on, "about the fact that I might have to, you know, take things slow."

At that moment, I got the reason for the call. He was trying to tell me why he felt he couldn't pursue our attraction right away. Not only that, he'd accomplished the impossible. He'd done this without making it sound as if he was dissing Khandi Kayne behind her back.

"I won't misunderstand, Alex," I said softly. "And just for the record, I think you're a really nice guy."

"I can't tell you how much I wish you

hadn't said that," Alex said at once. "I have it on very good authority that girls never fall for the nice guys."

"Guess you'll just have to see, won't you?" I asked.

"Guess so," said Alex Crawford. There was a second moment of silence. "So, I guess I'll see you tomorrow," he said.

"Alex," I said. "Can I ask you something?"

"Sure."

"Where's the closest Starbucks to campus? I owe Elaine a latte."

Late that night I stood in my bedroom, staring down at my open suitcases and listening to the sounds Old Mrs. Calloway's house made as it settled all around me. This was a phenomenon that had startled me at first. Apartments simply do not make those sounds. But now that I was used to it, I had to admit I kind of liked the way the house began to sigh and rustle as night came on. It was just one more thing that made it feel like the thing I'd never really had but had always secretly wanted. A home.

I think it was sometime in the middle of my third piece of pizza that I'd realized the truth.

Old Mrs. Calloway's house had won.

I was tired of being the girl who couldn't put down roots. Who moved from place to place without ever knowing why. What I wanted was to be the girl I'd so unexpectedly caught a glimpse of today. The girl I'd suddenly discovered I could be, if only I was brave enough to try. A girl who had a boyfriend who called her on the phone. Whose best friend lived right next door.

A girl who didn't have to figure out how to blend in, because she didn't have to. She fit. She belonged.

"Go on," Old Mrs. Calloway's house seemed to say. *"Take the first step. It's not so hard. You can do it, Jo."*

I stared down into the first of my suitcases. My very favorite sweater was folded neatly, right on top. This was the item of clothing I chose first when I was feeling warm and snuggly, just as it was my first when I was blue and needed cheering up.

Slowly, hardly daring to breathe, I picked it up, carried it across the room, and placed it in my bottom dresser drawer. As I did so, I heard the house sigh. I swear it was with approval.

I returned to the suitcase for the next item.

Six

When I think of the next few weeks, I'm reminded of a flashback sequence in a romantic film. The edges of the images are all slightly blurry. The colors are soft. The light, nostalgic and golden. I know it didn't really look like that. But that's the way it feels in my memory. Those were special days, carved out of time. Days during which it seemed nothing would ever change. Nothing would ever go wrong.

Ridiculous, of course. If there's one thing I ought to know, it's that change happens. And when it does, it's usually of the major variety.

The next change in my life happened on a Wednesday, if I recall.

The weather was the first thing that altered. Yes, all right. I know. Talking about the weather is generally considered a pretty lame thing to do. Get over it. But I have to tell you about the weather that day. It happens to be important.

It rained like hell.

I'd begun my tenure at Beacon in a stretch of warm, clear weather, which Elaine assured me wasn't typical at all. Spring in Seattle was cool and rainy, she kept insisting. I should not be packing away my turtlenecks and getting out my tank tops.

I didn't even try explaining that I'd barely *un*packed the turtlenecks. Though our friendship was definitely growing stronger day by day, I hadn't yet reached the point where I felt ready to talk about the way things had been before. There'd be plenty of time for that, I kept assuring myself. In the meantime, I was too busy enjoying the way they were now.

Fortunately for Elaine and me, the rain did let up long enough for us to make the trip home. We slogged along the wet side-walks, my feet getting wetter by the minute. I swear I heard them make these icky little squishy sucking sounds.

"That's funny," Elaine said as we rounded the corner of our street.

"What?" I asked, and promptly stepped into this enormous puddle.

"Your dad's home early. Isn't that his car in the drive?"

In that instant, I forgot about the rain. I forgot my wet feet. I forgot about every-thing but the fact that Elaine was right. My dad's car was in the drive. I know this doesn't sound like a big deal to you. All I can say is, to me, it was.

Once my dad and I establish a routine, we stick to it. That's one of the great unspoken rules of our lives. And the rule in Seattle was that Dad got home *after* I did. The reason for this was that he was work-ing in an office for the very first time.

Over the last couple of weeks, I'd devel-oped my own sub-routine until Dad got home. I went to Elaine's and we did our homework. If Dad worked late, sometimes I even stayed for dinner at the Goldens'.

That was the way things had been since we'd moved to Old Mrs. Calloway's house. I got home first. Dad got home second.

But there was his car, sitting in the drive. It was a change, and if there was one thing I knew, it was the way one change could lead to another. Not only that, in the case of Dad and me, *change* usually meant *change of location*. That thing I was so *D for Desperate* to avoid.

I gave what I sincerely hoped was a nonchalant shrug.

"Maybe he came home sick," I said. "Isn't there some weird flu thing going around? Listen, I'm going to go in and change my shoes before I come down with pneumonia. I'll be over in a few. If there's something up Dad-wise, I'll call."

"Okay," Elaine said.

There was a gust of wind, followed by a sudden return of the rain, full force. Elaine and I sprinted for our respective front doors. I heard hers slam behind her as she dashed inside. I stopped on the porch to tug off my wet shoes.

"Jo!" I heard a voice call.

I straightened just in time to see Alex dash up the front walk.

"I thought you had practice," I said.

"Cancelled," Alex said shortly. He made the front porch and pushed back the hood of the sweatshirt he had on beneath his letterman's jacket. His breathing was quick, as if he'd run all the way from school. "I tried to catch you guys but you'd already gone."

"Elaine's at her house," I said.

Alex gave an exasperated laugh and moved to put his hands on my shoulders, a thing that pretty much made me forget all about my dad's car in the drive. Apparently Alex had decided that the waiting period was over.

"I didn't sprint ten blocks to see Elaine," he said. "I came to see you. There's something I want to ask you, Jo."

"No, you can't borrow my math homework," I said.

"Shut up, you idiot," Alex said, giving me a shake. "I want you to go with me to the prom."

I opened my mouth, then closed it again. An action which no doubt made me look exactly like a fish out of water.

"That wasn't a question," I finally said.

Alex rolled his eyes. "Do you want to know why I like you?" he asked. "It took me a while, but I figured it out. It's because you're so impossible."

A laugh bubbled up and out before I could stop it.

"Impossible," I repeated. "What about annoying?"

"That too," Alex nodded. "You're impossible and annoying and unpredictable. Will you please go with me to the prom?"

"Aren't you worried about what will happen if I say yes?" I asked.

"Uh-uh," Alex shook his head. "I'm only worried that you'll say no."

"I'm not going to do that," I answered steadily. "Thank you, Alex. I'd love to go with you to the prom."

For a moment, he simply stood, his hands on my shoulders. "You'd better hold still," he warned.

"Why's that?"

"Because I'm going to kiss you now."

Words failed me. Which turned out to be a very good thing as, for the next few minutes, I needed my lips for something else anyhow.

The kiss ended and Alex eased back. There was an expression on his face I'd never seen before. Sort of startled and blank all at once, as if he'd just discovered something he hadn't expected but couldn't quite put a name to.

"Well," he said.

"Bet you say that to all the girls," I replied.

"I'm that obvious, huh?"

"Actually, no."

"Now who's being nice?" Alex said. He stuck his hands in his pockets. "So, I guess I'll see you tomorrow."

"Okay," I said. He turned, and I watched him sprint off down the walk. It was only then that I realized I was still clutching my sopping wet shoes.

Very smooth, Jo. No wonder the guy can't resist you, I thought.

Still feeling dreamy, I opened the front door and stepped into the hall. My eyes automatically sought out my mother's picture.

As if from a great distance, I heard my shoes hit the floor with a thud.

My mother's photograph was gone.

Seven

It only took me about twenty seconds to locate it. My dad was sitting on one of the living room couches, the one covered in fabric with these big hydrangea blossoms on it, cradling my mother's photograph between his hands.

No. Please, no, I thought. My chest was so tight it felt like I'd forgotten how to breathe.

Once we got to a new place, we never took Mom's picture down. The only times it even got touched were when I did the dusting, a thing that didn't happen all that often, and when Dad took it down to pack it. A thing that always meant . . .

"Forget about it, Dad," I said as I

finally remembered to close the front door. Actually, the word I'm looking for here is *slammed*. I slammed the front door. "Wherever it is, I'm not going."

My father looked up then. There was an expression on his face I'd never seen there before. Sad, yet determined, all at the same time. Though I didn't put it into words, I think I knew, right then, what he was going to say next.

"I understand why you feel that way, Jo-Jo," he said. "But I'm sorry to say there isn't any choice."

"Of course there's a choice," I snapped. "There's always a choice. You told me that yourself."

My father's eyebrows shot straight up. "I did not. When did I?"

"In fourth grade. When Arabella Swackhammer told everyone in Mrs. Mitchell's class the reason I was moving was because I'd been kicked out."

"Oh, thaat," my father said, drawing out the syllable the way people do when they're remembering something long forgotten. "You did something to get her back, didn't you?"

"Of course I did," I snorted. "I kicked her. What else? That night, after you'd gotten off the phone with the principal, you told me I could have expressed my anger in another way. You said I didn't have to resort to violence. There was always another choice."

"I never said *resort to violence*," my father protested. "I'd never be that pompous."

"The point I'm trying to make here, Dad," I said, "is that you told me I had a *choice*. There was always another *choice*. That's what you said. So now you're saying what? You lied to me when I was a child?"

My father scrubbed his hands across his face, the way he does when he's totally frustrated or exhausted. I admit seeing him do this gave me a pang. I am not a total monster. But it didn't give me a big enough one to back down.

"Come and sit down, Jo-Jo," my father said.

I shook my head, stubbornly. "No. Until I get my explanation, I'm staying right where I am. It's closer to the door, in case I decide I have to run."

My father looked into my eyes then.

And, in that moment, I swear to you I felt my heart stop.

"Josephine Claire Calloway O'Connor," Dad said, his voice calm and soft. "Please do me the courtesy of doing as I ask. Come over here and sit beside me. *Now.* You're not getting *any* explanation until you do."

What can I say? I went. Just as soon as my heart started back up. Not once in our lives had Dad ever done the full name thing. Not even the time I'd dumped an entire bowl of Neapolitan ice cream onto his brand-new laptop. Accidentally of course.

Plainly whatever was going on was important. More important than anything else had ever been before.

I walked over and sat down beside him. I tried to keep my distance. You know, to sort of get across the fact that I had obeyed his instructions under protest. Dad just reached over and pulled me closer, enfolding me in this big bear hug. He still had Mom's picture on his lap. I could feel the frame digging into my stomach.

The bear hug was one of Dad's best remedies when I was little. If I woke up at night, afraid because I didn't recognize my newest bedroom yet, crying because, just for a moment, I'd lost track of where I was, he'd come right in and hold me the same way he was holding me now.

It was either the best or the worst thing he could have done. The best because it really did make me feel better, just like it always had. The worst because I could feel the hot prick of tears, just behind my eyes.

"I really like it here, Dad," I said into his shoulder. "You know that, don't you?"

My father gave a sigh. "Of course I know that, Jo-Jo. If there was any way we could stay right where we are, I'd do it. But we can't. Not right now."

At that, I lifted up my head, and my father let me go. I scooted back a little, curling my feet up under me so I could face him.

"Does that mean we can come back?"

"I honestly don't know, sweetheart," my father replied. "I hope so, but it will depend on how things work out."

"What things?" I asked. "How come we even have to go at all?"

I could hear it then. The way my voice

slid perilously close to a whine. I hate people who do that. Whiners are my very biggest pet peeve. It was kind of depressing to discover that, under pressure, I might turn out to be one.

"It's because of something that happened a long time ago," my father said. Then he hesitated for a moment, as if trying to figure out the way to explain. To go on. That was the moment I decided to redeem myself for almost whining. In a funny sort of way, I suppose you could say it was the moment I grew up. Or at least, I started.

"Remember those bedtime stories you used to tell me? The ones you made up yourself?"

"Sure," my dad said, his face showing his surprise. He studied mine for a moment. "Okay," he said. "Okay, I gotcha, Jo-Jo."

He set Mom's picture beside him, on the far side. I scooted close to him again, and put my head back down on his shoulder.

"Once upon a time," my father began, "there was a man who had a daughter whom he loved very much. Life for the man was good, and he thought it would go on and on, just as it was. Then, one day, the man saw something he wasn't supposed to see. A thing that changed everything.

"He saw somebody die."

My head gave an involuntary jerk, popping up off my father's shoulder. Dad eased it back down again, smoothing my hair the way he'd done when I was a child.

"People die every day, for perfectly ordinary reasons," I ventured.

"True," acknowledged my father. "But there was nothing ordinary about what this man saw. The truth is, he witnessed a murder. Not only that, he saw the killer's face. A thing that turned out to be incredibly important. He was now almost the only person in the entire country who knew what this particular bad guy looked like.

"But the killer was clever. He got away. He was powerful and had many friends to help him. The police worried for the safety of the man and his daughter. So, together, they came up with a plan. The man and his daughter would move from place to place. That way, they could stay one step ahead of anyone trying to track them down."

"You mean they went on the run," I said. "Just like the killer did."

"I suppose you could say that," said my father after a moment. "Years went by, many more years than the man had ever imagined he would spend in that way. He stayed in touch with the police as he and his daughter moved from town to town.

"Then, one day, the man received a phone call. It was from the very same detective who had handled the case all those years ago. The detective told him the killer had been apprehended. At long last he would be tried for the murder, and the man would be called upon to testify.

"Before that could happen, though, there was a problem. A pretty serious one. Right before he'd been caught, the killer had discovered the whereabouts of the man and his daughter. Even though he was behind bars, the killer was still very powerful. He taunted the detective, saying he would go free because the man would never live to testify. The killer had put a price on his head."

At this, my head popped back up and stayed up. "Okay," I said, scooting back once more. "Wait a minute. Time out. You're telling me some psycho's after you?"

"I don't actually think he can be classified as a psycho," my father said. "He's just a really bad guy."

"I'm thinking *price on your head* is the thing to focus on here, Dad," I replied. "You're saying this guy wants you dead?"

My father nodded. "According to Detective Mortensen."

"And how does Detective Mortensen plan to protect you?" I inquired, trying not to hear the horrified panic in my own voice. Whatever story I'd thought my father might have told, whatever explanation he might have given for all our years of moving, this very definitely had not been it.

"And please tell me it's something better than having us move to Tacoma."

My father smiled then. "Actually he doesn't think we need to go that far. Detective Mortensen's theory is that the only way we'll be safe is if the killer believes that *he's* safe."

All of a sudden, I wished I were stupid. Because, if I were, then there might at least be some chance I was getting it wrong. That I'd misunderstood what my father was trying to tell me. My grade point average is 3.95. Unfortunately.

"You mean, *roaches check in, but they don't check out*, and we're the roaches, don't you?"

Incredibly, my father laughed. Then he pulled me back into his arms, his hug fierce. "I love you, Jo-Jo."

"I love you, too, Dad," I said. "And, for the record, I forgive you about the having-no-choice thing. Not only that, I think you're right."

"Just think of it as the exception that proves the rule," my father said.

We sat that way for a moment. Just the two of us together, the way it had been for almost as long as I could remember. "Do we have to go tonight?" I asked finally.

"We have to go tonight," said my father.

"And we have to leave everything behind. Whatever's going to happen needs to look like an accident, doesn't it?"

"That's right. It does. I'm sorry, Jo-Jo."

I almost did start to cry, then. Because I knew we both knew what my father had just done. He'd answered the question I hadn't wanted to ask right out loud. The one about what would happen to the picture of my mom. It seemed so unfair to have to leave it behind. As if we were losing her all over again when, in all honesty, once had been more than enough.

"Okay," I said. "Hand it over."

My dad reached to where my mom's photograph rested on the couch beside him and placed it into my hands. I got up and put the photograph in its shiny gold frame back where it belonged. Filling in the empty spot above Old Mrs. Calloway's mantel.

I looked at it for just a moment, then turned to face my father. He was looking at Mom's picture too. That same combination of expressions I'd seen earlier, sadness and determination, filling his face.

"So what's the plan?" I asked.

Eight

In the end, I did two things my father hadn't planned on.

I took the pink chenille bedspread, and I phoned Elaine. Not necessarily in that order.

The second was pretty much a necessity, as far as I was concerned, though it did take a while to convince my father. I think he actually put his hands on his hips.

"What part of *absolute secrecy* did you not understand, Jo?"

"You never said *absolute secrecy*," I shot right back. "You said it had to look like an accident. If I don't call Elaine, it won't. I *told* her I'd call or come over."

"Couldn't you just forget?" my father asked. "People do that, you know."

It was at this point that I put my hands on my hips.

"Dad," I said. "Will you just listen to yourself for a moment? I'm a teenager. I'm female. And you're seriously suggesting I might forget to use the phone?"

"It's just that Detective Mortensen . . ." my father began.

"Does Detective Mortensen know how close Elaine and I have gotten?" I ruthlessly cut him off. "Does he know I spend practically every afternoon at her house? Does he know she's already noticed your car is in the drive? She noticed it before I did, for crying out loud. I can't just drive off into the sunset without calling. She'll know something's up.

"I won't tell her anything, I swear. Just let me make the call."

"All right," my father gave in abruptly. "I don't like it, but we don't have time to argue. We need to be on the road in five."

"Thanks," I said. "I really appreciate this."

I headed into my bedroom and closed

the door. It was only then that I realized the truth: I had no idea what I'd say to Elaine now that I'd gotten permission to make the call. I mean, let's face it, the truth was very definitely out.

Mind racing, I pulled my cell phone out of my school pack and brought up my own personal phone directory, which contains all of two numbers: Elaine's and Alex's.

Oh, god. Alex, I thought. By this time tomorrow, he'd think I was dead, and there was absolutely nothing I could do about it.

You're probably wondering why I didn't just call him, too. And the truth is, I thought about it. But I also thought about the story my dad had just told. I was dealing with a potential life-and-death situation here. Specifically Dad's and mine. According to the story, Dad had pretty much spent his whole life making sure that I was safe. I couldn't pay him back by doing something that would risk him now.

Don't think about Alex, I told myself. *Don't think about the kiss you just shared and the fact that now you'll never go to the prom. If you do, you'll start to cry, and Elaine will know there's something wrong. You can make it up to Alex later. You can find a way.*

Blinking rapidly to hold back the tears, I punched the code for Elaine.

"It's me," I said when she picked up.

"Hey," she said. "What's taking so long?"

Fast. Do it fast, I thought. Sort of like pulling a tooth. It hurts like anything when you just haul off and yank, but it does make the pain go away sooner.

"Elaine," I said. "I can't come over."

"What? Why not?"

"My dad got this promotion at work," I heard myself say. I have no idea where this notion came from, but I was not about to look a gift inspiration in the mouth.

"That's why he came home early. To tell me all about it. The big boss wants to take us both out for dinner tonight. Apparently he's into getting to know the families of key employees or something."

"Well, that sounds potentially boring," Elaine remarked. "Do you know where you're going?"

Completely off the top of my head, I named the swankiest restaurant that I could think of.

"You'd better dress up," Elaine warned. "I think that's one of those places where, if you show up not wearing pantyhose, they give you some."

"That is so gross," I said. I pulled in a breath. It was now or never.

"SookayIguessI'llseeyoutomorrow."

I actually thought I sounded pretty convincing, except for the fact that I'd managed to completely defy the laws of physics and speak at the speed of light. Apparently Elaine remained unconvinced. A potentially ominous pause filled the phone.

"Jo, are you all right?" she finally asked. "Your voice sounds . . . I don't know . . . kind of funny."

"Of course I'm all right," I said quickly. "I'm always all right. I want you to remember that. As a matter of fact, I want you to promise me that you will."

"Okay," Elaine said, her own voice brisk and decisive. "That's it. What's going on?"

"Nothing," I responded. "But if something *were*, I'd be all right. I want you to remember that. I want to hear you say you will, and then I have to go."

"I don't understand," Elaine began.

"It doesn't matter," I cut her off. I took a breath. "Elaine, I realize we haven't known each other all that long, but I'm serious about this. You have to trust me. Please just say you know I'll be all right, no matter what you may read or hear to the contrary."

"I know you'll be all right no matter what," Elaine said.

"Jo, come on!" I heard my father call out. "It's getting late. We've got to go."

"I have to hang up. My dad's calling," I said into the phone.

"Jo."

"It's all right," I said. "It's going to *be* all right. I know you know this because you just said so. Don't try to call back. It won't do any good. I'll be in touch."

I disconnected, turned the ringer off, and put the cell phone back in my bag, all completely on autopilot. Then I just stood for a moment in my bedroom, taking several deep breaths, willing the tears not to fall. I'd never cried over leaving any place before. I didn't intend to start now.

"Jo!" my father called.

That's when I did it. I marched over to my bed and ripped that pink chenille bedspread right off it, wrapping it around my shoulders as if it were the world's most expensive fur stole. Then I left the room without a backward glance. My father was waiting nervously by the front door.

"What on earth?" he exclaimed when he saw me.

"Don't even try to talk me out of this," I almost sobbed. "I'll leave Mom's picture. I'll leave my friends. But the bedspread is going along for the ride. This is nonnegotiable. Take it or leave it."

"Okay," my father said. "Okay, Jo-Jo."

Without another word, he opened the front door. Then, with his arm around my shoulders, resting across that pink bedspread, we went out into the rainy Seattle night, side by side.

Nine

"Treacherous Curve Claims Father and Daughter"

That's what the headline in the local section of the paper read the following morning. And yes, it *is* just a tad bizarre to read an article detailing your own personal demise. Particularly when you, yourself, are safe and sound and drinking a grande nonfat latte at the time.

But you want to know the weirdest thing? The place Detective Mortensen had arranged for our "accident" to take place turned out to be right next to the restaurant where I'd told Elaine my dad and I were going. The intersection really is dangerous. Accidents happen there all the time, though generally not fatal ones. Without knowing it, I'd played right into our escape plans.

The escape itself was actually cool and constitutes the *techno* part of my story.

Before our supposedly fatal accident could take place, a switch had to be made. I mean, it was pretty obvious my dad and I couldn't actually *be* in the car. But because there existed the possibility that we were being watched, Detective Mortensen had to arrange for the switch to occur in a way that couldn't be observed. We couldn't just drive to the nearest gas station and switch cars.

So instead, we drove to the nearest car wash.

There, following the detective's instructions (relayed via my dad), I made a total fool of myself by throwing this very large and very childish fit about wanting to stay in the car as it went through the wash.

Eventually, of course, my dad gave in and let his bratty daughter have her way, but only after it was safe to assume that anyone in the whole world who might be watching had noticed us. We rode into the car wash, and two ace police drivers, selected for their resemblance to my father and me, drove back out.

We, meanwhile, had been transferred to the vehicle which had immediately preceded us into the car wash: a crummy-looking panel van which turned out to be filled with high-tech surveillance equipment. This transported us to what Dad and the detective referred to as the safe house, but which actually turned out to be a safe apartment.

Furnished, a thing I hardly need to tell you.

Once there Detective Mortensen and my dad filled me in on the plan from here on out. For security reasons, my dad would be confined to the apartment. Apparently Detective Mortensen had lobbied hard for this to be the case with me as well, but my father had absolutely put his foot down. I deserved a senior year, he said.

Which explains why I was able to die on Wednesday and still show up at school on Thursday morning, though not the same one, of course.

But first, I'd had a makeover.

Yes, I know.

Considering all the serious aspects of my situation, it does seem shallow of me to take a moment to discuss hair and clothes. But I can't have you thinking I was going to go around looking like, and calling myself, Jo O'Connor. That would have defeated the whole purpose of disappearing in the first place.

The first thing to change had been my name. I was Claire Calloway now. Another aspect of the back-to-school situation which had bothered Detective Mortensen, until I'd related the following story:

In seventh grade, I'd switched seats during math class with a classmate named Bonita Benson. We'd had a substitute and, as every student knows, substitutes are fair game. Unfortunately for me, the substitute was into class participation and had called on me. To be specific, she'd called on Bonita Benson, repeating the name about half a dozen times before I finally realized she meant me. A lack-of-reaction that had eventually resulted in both Bonita and I being sent to the principal's office.

I'll say this much for him. Detective Mortensen got the point at once. I was unlikely to forget I was Claire Calloway, as it was already a part of my name. Sort of like sticking to as much of the truth as possible when lying.

"You're sure you want to go through with this?" I suddenly heard the detective's voice say.

Detective Mortensen has this unusual way of speaking, very clipped and precise. An aspect of his personality totally at odds with the way he looks, which is pretty much a cross between a walrus and a bloodhound. His body is round, but his face is long and jowly.

According to my father, he's always looked like this, even when he was younger. He's been on the case since the very beginning. In fact, he was the one responsible for all those *Phone Calls of Mysterious Origin*.

Which only goes to prove that my theory about them was correct. It really *was* a guy.

I'd done my best to dislike Detective Mortensen. This seemed only reasonable

considering he was the one who'd insti-
gated me having to leave my entire life
behind. But the truth is, I couldn't quite
do it. It's kind of tough to dislike someone
who's making it their mission in life to
keep you alive.

Not only that, he and my father genuinely seemed to like one another. I'm
thinking all those phone calls over the
years resulted in a previously undiscovered
form of male bonding.

"Absolutely," I said with a great deal
more conviction than I actually felt. I set
the newspaper down on the breakfast table
and picked up a pair of black-framed
glasses. I slipped them on. Then I stood up
and did a quick turn around for Detective
Mortensen.

"What do you think?" I asked.

Detective Mortensen regarded me in
silence for a moment. "I'll say this much,"
he finally said. "It's a big change from Jo
O'Connor."

"That would be the point."

"You're sure you won't stick out too
much."

I shook my head, feeling the way the

new, long hair I'd chosen swished around my shoulders. I'd opted to become Claire Calloway by utilizing an entirely different sort of tactic than the ones I'd employed as Jo O'Connor. Rather than trying to fade into the woodwork, I'd decided to be easily identifiable.

The idea had come to me while reviewing my new schedule. Third period I was scheduled for journalism at my new school, Royer High. This had inspired me to adopt the artistic-intellectual look. Overnight, I'd become a member of the basic black crowd.

In preparation for my first day of school, I was now attired in a pair of black leggings, a pair of black Blunnies, and a soft black turtleneck sweater. The wig providing me with my new long hair (still brown) was held in place with a black headband. Funky, black-framed glasses completed the look, one I'd personally dubbed *intellectual chic*. I looked like the sort of girl who'd show up on open mike night at one of the trendy coffeehouses around Seattle, determined to inflict my poetry on others.

"There are two basic ways to fit into a new school if you don't want to attract a lot of attention," I explained now to Detective Mortensen. "The first is to try to be overlooked altogether. The second is to be easily identified. People are less likely to be curious about you if they think they already know who you are. Hence, the new look."

"Makes sense," the detective admitted.

"Hey, Jo-Jo," my father said as he came into the room. His eyes widened as he took in my appearance. "Wow, that's a change. All set to go?"

I took a moment to pick up my new black shoulder bag, slinging it across my body.

"I'm sorry, but I'm afraid you have me confused with someone else," I said. "My name is Claire. Claire Calloway. And you are?"

My father gave a startled laugh.

"And to think I was worried," Detective Mortensen commented. "Okay, Claire. It's time to roll."

I'd been able to walk to my old high school, but my new routine called for me to take the city bus to Royer High. As I walked the half a block to the stop, then stood waiting for the bus, I did a quick rundown of my cover story.

Claire Calloway was a transfer student from Buzzards Bay, Mass. I'd gone for a B name. I simply couldn't help it. I was an A student who planned to be an English major in college, a detail I thought would dovetail nicely with my new journalism assignment. My parents were divorced. I lived with my father.

And that was pretty much it. Beginning, middle, and end of story.

In the distance I could see the bus chugging its way along the street. Hear the squeal of the air brakes as it pulled into the various stops. I was one stop away from beginning my new life.

Okay, Claire. It's showtime, I thought.

The bus pulled up to my stop. The doors slapped open and I clambered on. A quick glance revealed an empty seat about a third of the way back. I paid the fare, accepted a transfer even though I didn't really need one, and sat down.

So far, so good, I thought. Detective

Mortensen had informed me that the stop for Royer was two stops beyond mine. As the bus continued its stately progression along the street, I shifted in my seat so that I was sitting sideways, my back against the inside wall of the bus, and surreptitiously began to eye my fellow Royer-ites.

They didn't look all that special, to be completely honest. By which I mostly mean they didn't look any different than the students anywhere else I'd gone. In addition to the business types heading to work, there were students of a variety of ages on the bus.

It was easy to tell the under- from the upperclassmen. Younger students tend to segregate by gender. Girls sit with girls, and boys with boys. The older students get, the more likely they are to sit together as couples, though usually even this was within a group.

Nothing different here, I thought.

That was when the bus made its next stop and *they* got on.

They were holding hands, a thing they managed to keep on doing as he paid the fare for both of them. She was a petite brunette. He, a tall and slightly lanky blond. Though they settled in immediately amongst their friends, they seemed to be inside their own little bubble. In a world all their own.

I could feel a horrible pressure begin to build inside my chest. *Alex and I used to look like that,* I thought. Or we could have, if we'd had more time.

The bus pulled away from the stop. I watched the way his head leaned over hers, his face alight with mischief as he teased her about something. She gave a laugh and grimaced, her face tilted upward.

He's going to kiss her, I thought.

That was when I looked away. I simply couldn't bear to watch. I'd worked so hard not to feel sorry for myself. Even insisting I start school right away, rather than waiting until next week. The truth, which I'd hardly been able to admit to myself, was that I wanted to keep busy. With too much time on my hands, I was afraid I'd start to brood about me and Alex.

What was he doing at exactly this moment? I wondered. Had he seen the paper? Did he know that I was dead? I'd sort of been able to prepare Elaine. But I hadn't been able to do anything for Alex.

With a wheezy screech of brakes, the bus pulled up at the Royer stop. One by one, my fellow students began to get off. I stayed right where I was. It was as if my entire body had suddenly frozen. Every part of me except my heart, which was beating painfully fast and hard.

I can't do this, I thought. *I can't start over. Not again. Not as Claire Calloway, not as anyone.*

The truth was, I didn't want to.

I'd already found my place, the place where I wanted to stay. The place where I belonged. It was at Beacon, with Alex and Elaine. It was living in Old Mrs. Calloway's house.

I knew it was the right thing to do, the only thing I *could* do, but I simply could not make myself get off that bus. I didn't want to start over, to move forward. How could I? I hadn't even had the chance to look back, to say good-bye.

That's it! I thought.

"You sure you're not getting off here, honey?" The voice of the bus driver suddenly interrupted my thoughts. Some bus drivers never talk to the passengers unless they absolutely have to. Others are kind of chatty, as if the fact that they're driving you from here to there makes them your new best friend, somehow. This driver was in the latter category.

"It's the Royer stop," she went on.

"Yeah, thanks," I said as I finally managed to stand up and shoulder my bag. I knew what I was going to do now. "Guess I just spaced there for a second."

"I hear you," she said. "Happens to me all the time."

"Not when you're behind the wheel, I hope," I said.

The bus driver laughed. "You have a good day now."

"Thanks. You too," I said. I clomped down the stairs. The doors whooshed closed behind me. With a roar of its engine, the bus drove off.

I waited until it had gone around the corner before I put my plan into action. That was all the time I gave myself to think it over. Any more and I was afraid I might chicken out and change my mind.

Before I could go forward I had to go back. Claire Calloway would never be able to live unless Jo O'Connor did something first.

She had to say good-bye to the guy she loved.

Ten

WARNING: The following chapter contains the introduction of IMPORTANT RULES which you will be asked to follow.

Not rules! you're no doubt thinking. To which I can only reply, I sympathize and I'm sorry. I wouldn't even bring the subject of rules up if I didn't consider it absolutely necessary. It's for your own good, honestly. I can't help thinking that I might not have made such an incredible mess of things if I'd just mastered a few basic concepts ahead of time.

Maybe I shouldn't even call them rules at all. Maybe I should call them guidelines.

Except for this first one though, which

is pretty hard and fast and you should follow it no matter what.

How Not to Spend Your Senior Year,
Rule #1:
If at all possible, don't pretend
to be something you're not.
Specifically, don't play dead.

Trust me. As this chapter is about to
reveal, I did it, so I should know.

Between the various city bus schedules,
it took a lot longer to get across town than
I had counted on. Then I deliberately
decided on a further delay. For obvious reasons, I wanted to try to see Alex alone. My
best chance of doing that would be following Drama, after morning break.

I'd settled in to wait at the Starbucks
not far from campus, the same one where
I'd bought Elaine the latte I owed her just
a few short weeks ago. It was just as I was
finishing the rest of the article about the
accident that had claimed the lives of
"Chase William O'Connor and his daughter, Josephine, commonly known as Jo,"
that the enormous flaw in the plan I'd so

suddenly cooked up occurred to me:

What if Alex wasn't in school at all?

Assuming he knew about the accident, it was perfectly reasonable to also assume he might stay home. What if I'd just come all the way across town for nothing?

No. That isn't Alex, I thought.

This was the guy who'd been class president for three years running. The only student in the history of Beacon High to be elected student body president by running unopposed. Alex was totally dedicated to student life. He'd show up at school, no matter what.

I polished off my latte and headed for the Little Theater, praying my disguise would hold.

It did, though I didn't know if it was because my makeover was brilliant, or simply that I timed my trip across campus so well I didn't meet anyone. I arrived at the Little Theater just before the class let out, then hid out in one of the bathroom stalls. Even if somebody came in, to the bathroom in general, I mean, I'd be safe behind my locked door.

I listened to the bell ring, counted to

one hundred. When the coast seemed clear, I slipped out of the bathroom and into the back of the darkened auditorium, easing my way over toward the righthand aisle. A ring of chairs was arranged on the stage, illuminated by the overhead stage lights.

They were empty except for the two occupied by Alex and Mr. Barnes.

At the sight of Alex, my heart gave a painful, lurching stumble. He looked absolutely awful. His face was pale and pinched.

"I just can't get it through my head," he was saying now. "I can't believe she's gone. How can she be gone? I just met her. I keep looking for her in the halls. I even went to meet her after first period English. It wasn't until I was standing outside the door that I realized what I'd done."

"That's all perfectly natural," Mr. Barnes said.

"You don't think it's unhealthy—that it means I'm in denial or something?"

Mr. Barnes shook his head. "Absolutely not. Disbelief is natural at first. It's all a part of the process. You just need to give yourself some time."

"It doesn't seem fair, somehow," Alex said. "I mean, Jo doesn't . . ." Abruptly he broke off. He dropped his head down into his hands. Mr. Barnes laid a hand on his shoulder.

"Why don't I just give you a minute, Alex," he suggested. "There's some paperwork I need to take care of in my office. Check in with me before you go. Don't rush things. I'm sure your next teacher will understand. We're all a little shook up today."

"Okay." I heard Alex's muffled voice through his fingers. "Thanks, Mr. Barnes."

"You're welcome," Mr. Barnes said. He stood up and made his way off the stage and up the center aisle of the auditorium. An oblong of light from the exit door shot down the aisle, then vanished.

Alex and I were all alone. More than anything in the world, I wanted to rush down to the stage and throw my arms around him. Tell him that he didn't have to grieve. I was all right. I was alive.

That was the moment I realized the awful truth. I looked like Claire Calloway, not Jo O'Connor.

I snatched my glasses off and stuffed them in my bag, in a total panic now. *My hair. What do I do about my hair?* I thought. I didn't even have a hat I could stuff it up under.

Onstage, Alex stood up. In another minute he'd be leaving. I'd miss my chance.

"Alex," I croaked. My voice was so weird and distorted, not even I recognized it. Not only that, it hadn't carried at all. I could tell from Alex's lack of reaction that he hadn't even heard me.

In that horrible moment, I flashed on this old film Elaine and I had gone to at one of the art houses so we could see it on the big screen: *Doctor Zhivago*. The plot is really long and convoluted and I have no intention of telling it to you now.

The thing that's relevant is that there's this one scene where Omar Sharif suddenly sees Julie Christie on the street. Or maybe it's a train.

Anyhow.

The point is, their two characters were once in love. But at this point in the film, she thinks he's dead. He tries to call out to her, to get her attention, only he gets all choked up. No matter what he does, he can't make her hear him. Eventually the vehicle pulls away without her seeing him. She never knows he's still alive.

The reason I'm telling you this is that, all of a sudden, I was seized with this incredible fear that this is what would happen to me. I'd try to call out to Alex, but he'd never hear me. He'd never know I hadn't really died.

I cleared my throat and tried again.

"Alex."

This time my voice came out way too loud. At the sound of it, Alex paused, one foot above the first step that would take him off the stage.

"Who is it? Who's there?" he called. He moved back into the center of the stage and lifted one hand to shade his eyes against the bright overhead light.

Well, you got what you wanted. You got his attention, I thought. *Now what?*

"Alex, it's me," I said. "It's Jo." Slowly, as if pulled by a giant magnet, I began to make my way toward the stage. What did it matter what I looked like? I could explain that. All that mattered was for Alex to know I was safe. I was alive.

"Alex, it's all right. I'm all right."

"Jo?"

Alex's voice must have risen an entire octave on that one syllable, hope and disbelief combined.

This is the right thing. I did the right thing, I thought.

At that exact moment, Alex's eyes rolled back in his head and he crumpled to the stage floor.

Eleven

"Well, now you've done it," I heard a voice say from the back of the auditorium.

I whirled, heart pounding. Fortunately for me, even through my shock, which was considerable, I recognized Elaine's voice.

"Don't do that. You scared me half to death."

"According to the paper, it's one hundred percent," Elaine said. She came swiftly down the aisle, her expression furious and fearful all at once. "What's going on? What have you done to Alex? I warn you, the explanation better be good, and I'd better hear it fast."

"Shut up! Just shut up a minute, will

you?" I snapped. "Get up here and help me make sure that he's all right."

I hoisted myself up onto the stage, then reached down a hand and pulled Elaine up beside me. Together, we knelt beside Alex. I felt for his pulse with trembling fingers. It was strong, though his skin felt clammy.

"It's okay. His heart is beating," I said. Then I did the thing I'd been trying to avoid ever since my dad first told me what had to happen. I burst into tears.

"Oh, geez," Elaine said. "Do you have any idea how hard it is to stay mad at you when you do that?"

She sat down beside me and put her arms around me. I rested my head on her shoulder. For a minute or two we sat, just like that.

"I guess the last few hours have been kind of tough," Elaine eventually said.

I made a sound that was somewhere between a laugh and a sob.

"You could say so. For the record, that was supposed to be Alex's line. He and I were supposed to be having a touching reconciliation right about now."

"Sorry it's only me," Elaine said, her

tone dry. "Allow me to recommend a less theatrical entrance next time."

"Look who's talking," I commented.

Somewhat more under control now, I sat back and began to rummage in my bag for the packet of tissues I always kept there. I had this horrible feeling my face was covered in tears and snot. That's how seriously I'd lost it.

"Are you okay?" Elaine asked.

I found the packet of tissues, extracted the top one, and blew my nose. Loudly. "Do I *look* okay?" I inquired.

"Well, no, not exactly," Elaine admitted. "But I'll say this much: You don't look dead."

A statement which might have made me start crying all over again, if it hadn't made me laugh.

"I am *not* dead," I said. "I just have to pretend to be."

"*What?*" Elaine said. "For heaven's sake, Jo, what's going on?"

"I don't have time to explain things now," I said as I fished my glasses out of my bag and put them back on. "I'm totally breaking all the rules by even being here. I probably never should have come back. It's just . . . I couldn't stop thinking about Alex."

"You didn't call him last night?" Elaine exclaimed, her voice incredulous.

I shook my head miserably. "I couldn't," I said. "It took everything I had to convince my dad to let me call you."

"I don't understand any of this," Elaine said. "Wait a minute. Why are you wearing glasses?"

"Meet me after school down at the Market and I'll explain everything, I promise."

The big farmers market near the waterfront was one of Seattle's biggest tourist attractions. You could pretty much count on it to be crowded no matter what. It would be the perfect place to meet unobserved.

"Where at the Market?" Elaine asked.

"That park that overlooks the water."

"The one where all the drunks hang out?"

"That's the one," I nodded. "Nobody's going to get close to us there. And if we are overheard, it will just sound like drunken ramblings. We'll blend right in."

"Okay. If you say so."

"Will you stay with Alex until he wakes up?"

"Of course I will," Elaine promised.

"What will you tell him?"

"How should I know?" Elaine shrugged. "It'll depend on what he says when he comes to. You should go, if you're going. I don't think it would be a good idea for him to see you again."

"All right, all right, you don't have to get all pushy about it."

I got to my feet, made a circuit around Alex, jumped down from the stage, and began to stomp my way toward the back of the theater. I was *not* going to start crying again, no matter how much I wanted to.

"Jo," Elaine suddenly called out.

I stopped, but didn't turn around.

"What?"

"I'm really glad you're not dead."

I turned back toward her then. In the glare of the stage lights, I could see tears slipping silently down her cheeks.

"Thanks. Me too," I said.

The last thing I saw before I went back outside was Elaine, bending tenderly over Alex.

Twelve

"You did *what*?" I all but shouted.

As prearranged, Elaine and I were keeping our rendezvous down at the Market. I'd spent the time in between wandering the downtown area, trying to adjust to my new Claire Calloway persona.

I'd developed a walk for her, stride slightly wider than my own. The boots I was wearing definitely helped with this. Head down, so that my hair fell forward. I also tried out a variety of ways she might speak, finally settling on the "when in doubt, use a big word to sound more intellectual" approach.

Somewhat to my surprise, I'd had a

good time. By the time Elaine and I hooked up, I was feeling much calmer. Much more focused. It had been a mistake to try and see Alex. I could see that now. I couldn't take the action back. But I could do my best to move forward. Surely the worst that could happen already had.

How Not *to Spend Your Senior Year,*
Rule #2:
Always expect the Spanish Inquisition,
no matter what anyone else does.

When he came to, Elaine told Alex he'd been visited by Jo O'Connor's ghost.

"I just don't get why you'd do such a thing," I said now.

"Well, gee, let me think," Elaine said, her tone defensive. "How about, because it seemed like the best idea at the time? It was Alex's idea, as a matter of fact."

"You are such a liar," I said. "It was not."

"I am not, and it was too," Elaine came right back. "Alex's first words after he woke up were something like, 'Did you see her?' so naturally I asked, 'Did I see who?' I wasn't going to admit I'd seen you until he did. Maybe he'd hit his head and had amnesia or something. How was I suppose to know?"

"Then what did he say?"

"Nothing," Elaine answered. "Not for a minute or two, anyhow. Then he looked me right in the eye and said he thought he must be more upset over your death than even he had realized. I asked him why. That was when he told me he thought he'd just seen your ghost.

"It took me about five minutes to convince him not to go straight to one of the special grief counselors the school brought in. That really would have blown the whole thing sky high."

"Thanks," I said as a huge pang of guilt swept through me. Grief counselors. For me. When I was still among the living.

"Don't mention it," Elaine replied. I could tell from her tone of voice that she was still a little miffed.

"No, really, I mean it," I went on. "Trying to go back and see Alex was a big mistake. I admit it. You performed damage control above and beyond the call of duty, particularly considering you didn't know what was going on. I want you to know I really appreciate it."

"I *still* don't know what's going on," Elaine reminded.

So I told her what I knew. After I'd finished, she was quiet for a really long time.

"You really think your dad's life could be in danger?" she finally asked.

"I honestly don't know," I said. Together, we watched a ferry glide across Puget Sound. The water and the sky above it were a brilliant blue. After the downpour of yesterday, we were being treated to one of those glorious spring days that make people decide to move here in the first place.

"But he seems to think so, and the detective who's helping us does for sure, so I guess I have to say the answer is yes," I went on.

Elaine shook her head, as if moving it around would help create the space necessary for all these weird new ideas to fit inside.

"So, maybe Alex thinking he saw your ghost will turn out to be a good thing," she suggested. "I mean, he's hardly likely to mention it to anyone, right? He'd be laughed right off all his various sports teams, not to mention removed from the student council in the blink of an eye. Big Men on Campus cannot be emotionally unstable. I think it's a rule."

"All very good points."

"So I guess you're sorry now you gave me such a hard time."

"Maybe I am," I said.

Elaine smiled. "So where are they sending you instead of Beacon?

"Royer," I replied.

"What's it like?"

"Ask me next week. By then I may have actually gone inside."

"What happens if the school calls your dad about today?"

I moaned and put my head in my hands. "I keep thinking this can't get any worse, and then it does. I never even thought of that."

Elaine laid a consoling hand on my shoulder. "It'll be all right," she said. "Isn't that what you told me?"

"I did," I said. "Guess it's time I started to believe it myself, huh? It just feels so weird. I've had to start over before, but never as someone else."

"Hey, I just thought of something," Elaine said. "What am I supposed to call you? You're not still Jo O'Connor, are you?"

"Elaine Golden, meet Claire Calloway," I said as I extended my hand. Obligingly, Elaine shook it.

"Calloway, that's kind of cool," she said. "Did you choose that because of the house?"

"Actually, Calloway was my mother's maiden name," I confessed.

Elaine's eyes widened. "Oh, wow," she said. "Is that weird or what? What if you're related to Old Mrs. Calloway?"

"I've wondered that myself."

Under her breath, Elaine began to hum the theme from *The Twilight Zone*. Though I might not have recognized it if I hadn't previously heard her attempt to carry a tune. Elaine is about as musical as a tree stump.

"Okay, that's it," I announced as I stood up suddenly. "If you're singing, I'm outta here."

"I was not singing," Elaine said, scrambling up after me. "I was humming. There's a difference."

"Not so long as there's a tune involved."

"Wait a minute," she said. "Jo—"

"Claire," I corrected. "Claire Calloway."

"Claire," Elaine said. "Tell me how we're going to stay in touch. You can't just show up, then disappear again. That's incredibly unfair, not to mention unacceptable."

"How about a secret phone signal or something?" I suggested. "I'll call, let it ring twice, then hang up. That'll be the signal that it's me. Then I'll call back and you can pick up. If you don't, I'll hang up without saying anything. I'll probably have to use a pay phone. They took away my cell."

"All the better," Elaine said. "That way we don't have to worry about caller I.D."

How did genuine fugitives manage? I suddenly wondered.

"How come you know about all this stuff?"

Elaine gave a sudden grin. "Must have been all those secret decoder rings I had when

I was a child. Okay, so, go to Royer tomorrow, then call me and tell me how it goes. It's Dennis's night to pick what's on TV. Chances are, he won't even hear the phone."

"Okay," I said. "I'll try."

"Don't try. *Do it,*" Elaine said. "Now go on, you'll miss your bus."

All of a sudden, I realized how much I didn't want to do it. Being Claire Calloway was a whole lot easier when Elaine was around.

"Keep an eye on Alex for me, will you?" I asked, in a feeble attempt to stall.

"Two eyes," Elaine said. "As often as I can spare them."

"Ha ha. Very funny. Elaine, I—"

"Don't," she said abruptly, holding up a hand. "Don't you dare say good-bye. Just call me Friday night."

Since I didn't seem to be capable of departing, Elaine was the one who turned to go. She got all of about ten paces before she turned back.

"Oh, by the way, Claire," she called.

"What?"

"Nice look."

For the first time that day, I smiled.

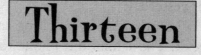

Thirteen

"Oh, yes, Claire Calloway," the journalism teacher, Mr. Hanlon, said. "We expected you yesterday morning."

"I apologize," I said. "I was delayed."

"Well," Mr. Hanlon said after a moment, when it became plain that this was the extent of the explanation I planned to offer. "You're here now. That's what counts. How are you at copyediting?"

"Proficient but not foolproof."

"I think that will do," Mr. Hanlon said with just the hint of a smile. He pointed across the room to a slightly round guy in jeans and a striped shirt. "Go see Rob."

It was my third period as Claire

Calloway, newest student at Royer High. So far, things were going well, if I didn't count the fact that, for some unknown reason, my glasses kept slipping down my nose. Maybe I'd bent them in all the excitement of yesterday.

I'd begun the day by catching my very first break. The school did phone to verify that Claire Calloway would, indeed, be starting classes, but my dad was in the shower and I was the one who picked up the phone. I'd apologized for the mix-up in dates, assured the school secretary I would be present that day, then asked for her name so I could thank her in person when I arrived.

Jo O'Connor never would have done this. But it seemed to fit Claire Calloway's personality nicely.

The first part of the day had been devoted to the usual new school details. Locate the locker. Fumble with the combination. Figure out where the classrooms are. This was more difficult for Claire than it had ever been for Jo. She hadn't had the chance to commit the school layout to memory ahead of time.

By the time I hit third period and journalism, though, I was feeling pretty good. I was beginning to know my way around. Claire Calloway wasn't attracting too much attention, and nobody at Royer seemed to even know who Jo O'Connor was.

Settling my big, black bag more securely on my shoulder, I set off across the room to face my newest challenge. Introducing myself to Rob.

Even from across the room Rob reminded me of the human version of a tea kettle. Slightly round and sputtering, apparently about to boil.

"I do not have *time* for this," he wailed, waving a sheaf of papers in the air as I wove my way between the desks. "How *dare* Shawna be out sick today. Doesn't she understand we're on a deadline?"

"I'm sorry to interrupt," I said. "But are you Rob?"

"Of course I'm Rob," he sputtered without turning around. "Who else would I be?"

"Well," I answered in Claire Calloway's slightly prissy, intellectual voice. "Perry White does come to mind."

Rob spun toward me, his eyes wide. "A mystery woman in black who knows the name of Clark Kent's editor," he said. "Please tell me your name is Lois Lane."

"Sorry. Claire Calloway," I said with a smile as I surreptitiously tried to edge my glasses back up my nose. "Mr. Hanlon asked me to see you. He said something about copyediting?"

"What makes you think you know anything about copyediting?" Rob barked.

Oh, goody. He's testing me, I thought.

"Experience," I answered calmly. "Not for a paper, I admit. But my uncle is a researcher." The substitution in family member rolled easily off my tongue. "I edit his reports all the time. Both he and his clients have always been more than satisfied with my work."

Oooh. Good job, Claire.

Rob thrust the stack of papers he was holding toward me, pulled a red pen from behind his shirt pocket, and slapped it down on top.

"Pleased to meet you, Claire Calloway," he said. "You're hired."

★

Copyediting is definitely not a task for everyone. Most people would find it pretty boring. You have to know a lot about writing, but you don't actually get to *be* a writer. You double check things like facts, quotes, and foreign word usage. Grammar, punctuation, spelling.

Maybe it was my father's legacy coming out in me, but the truth is, I kind of liked it.

I found an empty desk, settled in, and got to work, ignoring the curious looks of the students around me. There'd be time to concentrate on them later. Right now I needed to focus on winning over Rob.

Over the years I'd edited my dad's reports, I'd developed my own routine. Of course. I'd read first for sense and to see if anything glaringly wrong jumped right out at me. Then I'd read again, more slowly, making corrections as I went along. I'd make a note of anything I thought I needed to look up.

It took me most of the period to work my way through the stack. The piece at the bottom of the pile was the most impressive. No corrections at all.

"How's it going?" a voice above my head asked. A guy's voice. *Not Rob,* I thought. Probably one of the writers, wondering how his article had faced up to the red pen.

"Fine, thank you," I said, putting the pen cap back on.

"All done?"

It looks that way, doesn't it? I thought.

"That would be correct," I said aloud.

"Fast work," the guy commented. "Shawna never got done in just a single period."

At that, I finally looked up and met his eyes. They were dark, just like his hair, both brown but darker than mine. He was tall and lean. Something about the way he was holding himself made me think he might be a runner.

Tall, dark, and artistic, I thought. I wondered if Royer assigned *Wuthering Heights.* If so, all the girls probably had a Heathcliff complex about this guy. The thought made me smile.

Just great, I thought. *Now he'll think that's for him.*

"I'm not Shawna," I pronounced with a scowl.

"I can see that," he answered. "You said Claire, right? Where'd you say you were from?"

"I didn't," I said. "But it's Buzzard's Bay, Mass. And you are?"

"Mark London."

I should have known, I thought. His was the article that hadn't needed a single correction, a thing he no doubt knew quite well. Right after whiners on my list of pet peeves come people who constantly need to have their egos stroked.

By which you'll gather that, like Alex, Mark London made a big first impression. Unlike Alex, however, my first impression of Mark wasn't all that positive.

"Pleased to meet you," I said as I got to my feet, even though I wasn't. "If you'll excuse me, I'd better get these to Rob."

"Okay," Mark said. He let me step around him, then trailed along behind.

"Hey, Lois Lane," Rob said when I placed the papers on his desk. "You're done. Way to go." His eyes flicked behind me to where I could feel Mark London hovering just beyond my shoulder, then back to my face. "How many corrections for the article on the bottom of the stack?"

"You mean the one with Mark's name on it?" I asked. A hush fell across the room, as if some cosmic deity had just turned the volume down. "None."

"You're sure," Rob urged. "No chance you could be wrong."

Part of me was hating being in the spotlight. Another part decided it was a fine moment to establish Claire Calloway's personality once and for all.

"Of course there's that chance," I said, my tone priggish, as if he'd offended me. "I'm human. I make mistakes, just like *everybody else* does."

I heard a quickly hushed snicker whip around the room. *Good,* I thought. Everyone was getting the fact that Claire Calloway was smart and not a pushover. Also, she was not intimidated by the likes of one Mark London.

"In the case of the article in question, however, I honestly don't think I've made an error. Why? Is there a problem?"

"The article in question," Rob echoed, his face suffused with delight. "Lois, I think I love you."

"I'd appreciate it if you'd call me by my name," I said.

"Hey, Rob, the other editions are in," a voice suddenly called out.

"Great," Rob said. "Didn't that girl who just died go to Beacon? Let me see that one first."

I felt as if I'd taken a rabbit punch right in the head. *That girl who just died. That's me,* I thought.

"Wait a minute," I said, actually turning to Mark London in desperation as Rob sputtered off. "What one from Beacon? What's he talking about?"

"We read all the other school papers every week," Mark said simply. "Rob thinks it helps us stay competitive. It's no big deal. Actually, it's usually pretty boring."

Bet that won't be a problem today, I thought. As it turned out, I had no idea how right I was.

"You guys are not going to believe this," Rob's voice said. He held the *Beacon Banner* up over his head. I could read the headline clear across the room.

DEAD STUDENT WALKING?

"Well, that's tacky," a girl standing close to Rob said.

Without warning, I felt my legs give out. I sat down at Rob's desk, abruptly.

"Hey," Mark said. "Are you all right?"

"Yeah," I managed. "Fear of being unable to stay competitive or something."

"Listen to this," Rob said. "'I saw Jo O'Connor's ghost,' claims student body president, Alex Crawford."

There was a moment's startled silence.

"The student body president," Mark commented over the sudden outburst of excited talking. "Pretty reputable source." With a last glance at me, he moved to Rob's side.

Rob set the paper down on the nearest desk. Although most of the rest of the class crowded around him, he continued to read aloud.

"'Reeling from the shock of popular student Jo O'Connor's death in a traffic accident just a little over twenty-four hours ago . . .'"

Popular student? I thought. Not the way I would have described myself. Maybe they were just saying nice things about me because I was dead.

"'. . . students at a grief-counseling session were treated to a second shock when student body president Alex Crawford revealed he had received a visit from Jo's ghost,'" Rob read on.

Guess Alex went in for counseling after all, I thought.

Rob read on:

"I was sitting in the Little Theater, trying to, you know, come to terms with what had happened," Crawford claims, "when suddenly I heard a voice. It called my name. When I asked who was there, the voice said, *'Alex, it's me. It's Jo.'"*

Crawford admits events are a little hazy after that, as it appears he literally passed out from the shock. He was discovered by Jo O'Connor's closest friend and next-door neighbor, fellow senior Elaine Golden. When asked by this reporter whether or not she'd seen anything, Ms. Golden provided a prompt and emphatic denial.

"'I didn't see Jo O'Connor's ghost,'" she said. "When asked her opinion on Alex Crawford's experience, Ms. Golden's only comment was, 'No comment.'"

Way to go, Elaine, I thought. She'd found the way to tell the truth and hide it, all at the same time.

The article went on to indicate that full details of the fatal crash, which had also claimed the life of the driver of the vehicle, Jo O'Connor's father, could be found on page five. Related articles on the potential veracity of spirit manifestations could be found on page four. Information regarding various memorial activities being contemplated in honor of Jo O'Connor was on the back page. For a collection of photos commemorating Jo's all-too-brief life at Beacon High, readers were instructed to turn to page two.

In other words, you could pretty much say the entire edition of the paper was about me, in one way or another.

"Let's see the photographs," Mark suggested as he peered over Rob's shoulder.

Uh-oh, I thought.

Obligingly, Rob turned the page. *I should go over there,* I thought, if only for purposes of camouflage. The trouble was, my legs still didn't seem to want to function. I couldn't decide if this was a good thing or a bad one. If my legs had worked, chances were excellent I'd have given myself away by running.

I slid my glasses off, set them on the desk, and massaged my temples. All of a sudden, my head was pounding.

"She looks nice," I heard a voice say. I lifted my head to find Mark London's eyes on me.

"Omigod," Mark suddenly exclaimed.

"What?" Rob asked.

"Look at the pictures,"

"I'm looking at them," Rob said. "So?"

"Now look up," he instructed, pointing. At that moment, I felt a sudden kinship with a rabbit caught in the glare of headlights. For a second or two I wondered if maybe I *had* died, after all.

If this wasn't hell, I sure didn't know what was.

Mark was pointing, and the entire room was looking, right at me.

"Holy cow," Rob said.

Do something! my mind was screaming. *Don't just sit there!*

I snatched my glasses back up, cramming them onto my face. "What?"

"I don't know how to tell you this, Claire," Mark London said. "But you're an absolute dead ringer for Jo O'Connor."

Fourteen

At his words, I'm pretty sure every ounce of blood drained right out of my face.

Great, I thought. *Now I look like a ghost.*

"Dead ringer," I said. "Ha ha. Very funny. Too bad there isn't a Pulitzer for humor. You could be the youngest person ever to win the prize."

"Actually he does have a point," the girl standing beside him suddenly spoke up. "You have the same shaped face. Same color eyes."

"Has everybody just gone insane?" I inquired. "My eyes are *brown*. That's only the most common color there is. Remember Genetics 101?"

"Okay, well what about this?" Mark challenged, really getting into the comparison thing now.

"According to the article, Jo O'Connor was killed on . . ." Quickly Mark flipped back to the front page. ". . . Wednesday the eleventh," he read aloud. "Your first day here is Friday the thirteenth. That's an interesting coincidence, don't you think?"

"Fascinating," I replied. *What on earth am I going to do?* I wondered. Then I remembered that old saying. You know the one. The best way to defend yourself is to come out swinging. Something along those lines.

"So, let me see if I've got this straight," I said as I forced myself to my feet, relieved that my lower body had decided to help out and hold me up. "What's your name?" I asked, focusing on the girl who'd pointed out the shape of my face.

"Diane," she said.

"Okay, Diane. You think I look just like this girl who died. Would that be before or after the accident?"

Rob gave an explosive snort of laughter.

"Well, before, of course," Diane answered, her tone sulky.

"Great. Now we're really getting some-where," I went on. "I'm a dead ringer for a dead girl. Not only that, Mark's just pointed out the remarkable coincidence that I started here a mere two days after she died. This seems highly suspicious, I agree. So what if the truth is that this girl—what's her name again?"

"Jo," Rob said. "Jo O'Connor." I could tell by the look on his face that he was really enjoying himself.

"What if this girl named Jo O'Connor didn't really die? What if I'm her, only I don't know it? I call myself Claire Calloway because I've sustained major head injuries and don't know who I am anymore. Never mind that I came complete with tran-scripts. Those can be faked, as we all know.

"Of course, it *is* harder to overlook the fact that I walked away from an accident that killed one other person without a single scratch on me. But I'll bet if we give Mark enough time, he can come up with a conspiracy theory to cover that pesky little anomaly, thereby clinching his spot on the staff of the *National Enquirer*."

"Well you don't have to get all bent about it," Diane said.

A spontaneous round of laughter erupted, effectively putting an end to the discussion. Even Mark joined in, though I noticed he kept his eyes on me, their expression somehow managing to be both thoughtful and sharp all at the same time.

"Wait a minute. I am just about to be brilliant!" Rob suddenly exclaimed.

Great. So precisely what I do not need, I thought.

"I don't suppose I could talk you out of it," I said aloud.

"The exchange starts next week, doesn't it?" Rob said, completely ignoring me and turning to Mark.

Mark's eyebrows shot up. He nodded. "On Monday."

"The what?" I asked. Not that I was really all that sure I wanted to know.

"The *exchange*," Rob said once more. "The inter–high school journalism exchange. It's happening with all the high schools in town. One staff member from each paper is trading places with their counter-part at another, then writing about what it's like to be a senior somewhere else.

"It's sort of a citywide special interest story: 'How the Other School Lives.' Kind of a cool idea, if I do say so myself."

"That's because you thought of it," somebody commented.

Rob grinned. "Hey, can I help it if I know a good idea when I think of one? My point is this: Beacon is our partner in the exchange! We're about to become the envy of every other high school paper in town. I say we send Claire to do the exchange and report on the ghost sightings at the same time!"

"Now wait just a minute," I began.

But by now Rob was off and running. He began to sputter around the room like a general planning an elaborate campaign.

"I should send a photographer along too," he said. "Just for a couple of days or so. It will be important to capture all those initial candid encounters."

"I thought Mark was going to do the exchange," Diane spoke up.

Rob's sputtering stopped abruptly.

Saved, I thought.

He couldn't send me instead of Mark.

My guess was he was their star reporter.

"Mark should definitely be the one to go," I said.

"I agree with Rob. Claire should go," Mark said at the same time.

"There, see? Mark agrees," Rob said.

"You guys cannot be serious," I said, appalled. "You're going to send me over there because you think I look like that girl who died. How creepy can you get? Not to mention, how tabloid."

"It is not tabloid," Rob protested. "It's a perfectly legitimate way of getting a story. The fact that you're a dead ringer for this girl who died actually makes it all more poignant."

"Could we please dispense with the phrase 'dead ringer'?" I interrupted.

"If I might put my two cents in," Mr. Hanlon suddenly spoke up. At the sound of his voice, every head in the room turned toward him. I wasn't quite sure when he'd come out of his office, but I was glad he had.

He'll put a stop to this, I thought.

"I think that, if handled with sensitivity, Claire's resemblance to the Beacon student could actually bring out some unusual insights," Mr. Hanlon said.

At his words, I felt my heart sink like a stone. *How can this be happening?* I thought.

"But I think that it's important not to lose sight of the original purpose of the exchange: to provide insight into what it's like to attend a different high school. Having the chance to write an article at a school where people are grieving does present a unique opportunity. And Claire's resemblance to the student who died might actually enable her to get people to open up in a way they might not otherwise.

"But the fact that she resembles the friend they've lost could also be a two-edged sword. There may be some people who can't handle the resemblance, who resent Claire for it. She should only go if she feels the situation is one she can handle. She is brand-new to the paper, and our school, after all. Mark does have more experience."

"So, what do you think, Lois Lane?" Rob asked. "Are you up for a challenge?"

"Don't think that's going to work," I said. "You're not going to get me to say yes just because I don't want to back down from a challenge."

From across the room I saw Mark London grin. A thing that actually made him look almost human. "Nice way to call a bluff."

"Thanks," I said dryly. "I've been waiting for your seal of approval all morning."

"Why don't Claire and I work together?" Mark proposed, his grin growing a little wider. "She can start the exchange while I get going on some background. If Claire discovers she can't handle things, we can switch."

Talk about a nice way to call a bluff, I thought. Mark's proposal was so reasonable, he'd pretty much given me no way out. Not only that, he'd added something. While I was busy coping at my old school, he'd be snooping around behind my back, a far-from-thrilling prospect.

"It's a good suggestion," Mr. Hanlon said. "But my feeling is that to be truly in-depth, we need one person's point of view throughout the entire article. If Claire feels she can handle the additional complications her appearance may present, fine. She can take the assignment. If she prefers not to, Mark will go as originally planned."

"Well, Claire? What do you say?" Rob asked.

Once again I could feel every single eye in the room upon me.

There's no way I can turn this down, I thought.

If I did, the inevitable would happen. People would start to wonder why. There would be whispering. Gossip. And that might lead to the asking of questions I couldn't afford to answer. It would be bad enough to have Mark snooping around in Jo O'Connor's background.

The only way I could get out of it was to break a leg. Or possibly a neck, preferably Mark's or Rob's.

"All right," I said. "I'll take the assignment."

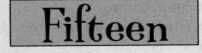

Fifteen

How Not *to Spend Your Senior Year,*
Rule #3:
No matter how dire things get,
do not panic.

It will only make a bad situation even worse. Besides, by the time you've reached the hit-the-panic-button stage, it's way too late. Nothing you do will make a difference anyhow.

This is a phenomenon known to the ancients as irony. You may be more familiar with the contemporary expression of this concept: Life sucks.

Particularly weekends.

He'd only been confined to the apartment a couple of days, but already my dad was pacing like a caged tiger. I vacillated between depression over what had happened the previous week, and terror over the week to come.

Why had Alex talked about seeing my ghost? It seemed completely unlike him. The only reason that made sense was that he was incredibly upset. A thing that made me feel incredibly guilty. I'd tried to make him feel better and had only made things worse.

By the time Monday morning rolled around I was completely exhausted. It was almost a relief to stand at the bus stop as usual, even though I was pretty sure I was being transported straight into disaster. Anything was better than sitting in the apartment while my thoughts circled like hungry vultures.

"You're Claire Calloway, aren't you?"

I turned to see a girl who looked vaguely familiar standing at the stop.

"That's right," I said. "I'm sorry, do I know you?"

"Not really," she acknowledged with a

friendly smile. "I'm Julie Banks. We have first period history together. Diane Peterson is a friend of mine."

"Diane from journalism class?" I asked as I began to make the connection.

The bus pulled up to the stop. Julie and I climbed on and she sat down beside me.

"That's right," she nodded. "Diane says you're going to do that exchange thing over at Beacon. Bet that will be freaky for all concerned."

You have absolutely no idea, I thought.

"I tried to make that point," I admitted. "Everybody else seems to think it's a good idea, though. As a result, I didn't get very far."

"When do you start?"

"This afternoon, I think. Mr. Hanlon will give me the details in class this morning."

Julie was silent for a moment. "I saw that girl's picture in the paper. You really do look like her, you know."

Here we go again, I thought.

"I do know that," I said. "That doesn't make us the same person."

"Of course it doesn't," Julie said at

once. "I just—I think you're handling it really well."

She's trying to be nice, Jo-Claire, I thought. *You might try cutting her a little slack.*

"Thanks," I said. "So, give me the scoop on Mr. Patterson, the history teacher."

For the rest of the trip to school, Julie was happily diverted by my clever change of subject.

"So, we're all clear about the way this works, right?" Mr. Hanlon asked.

I nodded. The actual logistics of the inter–high school newspaper exchange were pretty straightforward. For the next several weeks I'd attend a variety of Beacon classes in the morning, then travel across town to Royer during my lunch break and attend my regularly scheduled classes in the afternoon. My Beacon counterpart would do just the opposite, thereby allowing each of us to be a part of our exchange school's newspaper staff.

The one exception would be today, when I'd head to Beacon just as soon as my meeting with Mr. Hanlon was over. So far, he'd voiced only one concern. I didn't have my own transportation.

"It will make for a hectic schedule for you, Claire," Mr. Hanlon said. "You'll probably end up spending most of your lunch period coming across town."

"I'll be fine, Mr. Hanlon," I assured him. "I can always eat on the bus. And riding is usually easier than fighting crosstown traffic."

I'd heard my dad say that. I hoped it would make me sound as if I knew what I was talking about.

Mr. Hanlon was silent for a moment, his expression thoughtful.

"You're sure you still want to go through with this?" he asked quietly. "I sensed some genuine hesitation from you last week. This transportation issue could provide you with a way out."

"Without losing face, you mean," I said.

"Something like that," he acknowledged with a smile.

I hesitated for a moment. I was tempted, I admit. But I couldn't quite see myself backing out now. I'd still face the same questions that I'd feared last week.

"To tell you the truth," I said, "there *are* things about this assignment that make me uncomfortable. But I can also see that it's a unique opportunity. If I don't take it, I'll probably look back and be sorry. I'm willing to work around the transportation issues if you are."

"All right," Mr. Hanlon nodded. "Fair enough. Remember that you can come to me with any concerns."

"Thanks, Mr. Hanlon," I said.

"You're welcome, Claire." He shook my hand. "Good luck."

I hope you'll never know how much I need it, I thought. Tucking my transfer papers into my bag, I headed out of the school and toward the bus stop. I was just about to cross the street when I heard a voice call out:

"Hey, Calloway. Wait up!"

Calloway. That's me! I realized.

A moment later Mark London thundered up beside me. For a moment my heart gave a surge of hope. Maybe he'd spent the weekend regretting his decision. Now he was going to plead with me to change my mind. I'd pretend not to, then give in at the very last moment. All problems solved.

"Hello, London," I said, deciding two could play the last name game. "Change your mind?"

"Nope," he said, his voice disgustingly cheerful. "I just saw Mr. Hanlon. He was kind of worried that you didn't have a ride. How come you don't have wheels?"

"I just moved here," I said. "Riding the bus is a good way to get to know the city. Besides, taking public transportation is more socially responsible."

Mark smiled. Once again, I couldn't help but notice how much nicer he looked when he did that.

"So, here's what Hanlon and I worked out. I'll drive you over and pick you up. For today, at least. After that we can see how it goes."

"I appreciate the offer, but it's completely unnecessary," I said. "I'm a high school senior, not a kindergartner who needs to have her hand held."

Mark's eyes did this funny thing just then. They flicked down to my hand, then back to my face. I felt this *zing* shoot straight up my spine.

"Okay," he said. "But don't you even wanna know what kind of car I drive?"

I gave up. Sometimes it's easier than arguing.

"Is it the kind that requires me to pay for gas?"

"Not today."

"Then I love it."

"So," Mark said as he piloted his car, which turned out to be a vintage VW Bug, through the Seattle traffic, "how do you like it here so far?"

"It's okay." I shrugged. I could feel him give me a sidelong glance as we moved through an intersection. "All right," I confessed with a quick laugh. "I'll admit it. I love it."

"Bet it's a pretty big change from Buzzard's Beak," Mark commented.

"Buzzard's Bay," I said, knowing he was well aware of what the correct name was. "But you're right."

"How come you moved here in the first place?" Mark asked. We pulled to a halt at a stoplight.

"My dad's job."

"Which is?"

"Which is none of your business," I said, without heat, as the light turned green. "Could we please dispense with the interview portion of the program? You're making me wish I'd taken the bus after all."

"Okay, okay," he responded. "Can't blame a guy for trying."

"Who says?" I asked. Mark chuckled. We drove for several blocks in silence.

"You feeling all right about today?" he finally asked.

I shrugged and nodded all at the same time. "I guess so."

Mark gave me a second sidelong glance. "Would you get all bent out of shape if I offered some advice?"

"Probably," I said. "Something tells me you're willing to overlook that fact, though."

"And here I thought I was a man of mystery."

I decided to let that one slide.

Mark braked to allow a pedestrian to cross the street, then negotiated a corner. It was a point in his favor that he wasn't one of those guys who thought he could impress a girl by flashy driving.

"So," I said as the car began to pick up speed. We were traveling along a main arterial that bordered the water now. "Are you going to give me that advice or aren't you?"

"Well, since you asked . . ."

I laughed before I could stop myself. "You're a pain. You know that, London?"

"Of course I know it," he said. "My parents tell me so all the time. It's just that I was thinking it might be easiest to do the hard stuff first when you get to Beacon."

Like any of it is going to be easy, I thought. But then, I did face challenges he didn't know about.

"What do you mean, the hard stuff?"

"The hardest interviews," he said. "The boyfriend, Alex Crawford. And the best friend—What was her name?"

"Elaine," I said. "Elaine Golden."

"That's good," he nodded. "You're right there with that name."

"I did some homework over the weekend," I answered shortly. "You're not the only one who likes to do a good job, you know. Why do you think I should do those interviews first?"

"So you won't let the potential freak

149

factor of doing them at all get blown out of proportion. I'll bet you're already worried about them, aren't you?"

"What if I am?"

"You see?" Mark said. "There you go. Defensive already. That's why you should do the hard ones right off. The freak factor will plummet, and it'll be easier to focus on the overall assignment."

It was good advice, I had to admit.

"Thanks," I said. "That's good advice, and I'll keep it in mind."

Surprise flickered across his face. *He didn't expect me to admit he'd been right,* I thought. For some reason, this made me like him a little better.

"Don't mention it," Mark said.

"I do have a question, though," I continued as he pulled into the Beacon High parking lot.

"Shoot," Mark said.

"How come you're being so nice to me all of a sudden?"

He gave a bark of surprised laughter. "Hey," he protested. "I can be nice."

"Okay," I said agreeably. "But why *are* you?"

He was silent for a moment. He switched off the car, pulled the keys from the ignition, then, suddenly serious, turned toward me.

"Let's just say I'm returning the favor."

"When did I do you a favor?" I asked.

"Last week. That thing about not finding anything wrong with my article."

"I didn't do anything," I said. "There was nothing to find."

"Exactly," Mark said. "But you didn't pretend there was. That's what Shawna always does. She . . ." Abruptly frustrated, he ran his hand through his hair. "I'm trying to think of a way to say this that doesn't make me sound completely full of myself."

"You may as well stop trying," I suggested. "I already think that."

He expelled a quick breath and shook his head as if chastising himself for giving me the opening.

"Are you sure you're not a kindergartner? You've got all the makings of a first-class brat."

I smiled sweetly. "Thanks so much."

He pulled in a breath. "See, here's the

deal," he said. "I'm good at what I do on the paper. I *want* to be good at it. Being a journalist is what I want to be when I grow up. Some people have a hard time with that. They think I want to be good to show them up, when the truth is, it doesn't have anything to do with them at all."

"So they try to prove you're not as good as you think you are," I filled in softly.

Mark nodded. "But you didn't do that," he said. "Instead, you did your assignment. I appreciate that, and I figured it meant I owed you one. Hence, the giving of advice."

"So few people actually use the word hence in conversation these days," I said. "It's kind of nice to meet a guy who doesn't regard English as a second language, even when it's his first."

Mark laughed again, the sound open and delighted. "You know what, Calloway? You just may be all right."

"Save it," I said with a laugh of my own as I opened the car door and got out. "Advice I may take. Flattery will get you nowhere."

"Who says it was flattery?" Mark inquired, getting out in his turn.

"What are you doing?" I asked.

"What does it look like I'm doing? I'm getting out of the car."

"I can see that," I said. "Why?"

"So I can walk you to the office and see what kind of reaction you get," Mark said simply, his eyes dancing with wicked laughter. "Why else do you think I offered you a ride in the first place?"

I should have known, I thought.

"London, I can't believe you are such a jerk."

"That's only because you barely know me, Calloway," he said as he came around to my side of the car. "We can fix that." Before I knew quite what he intended, he reached down and captured my hand.

"You know, I think I might want to hold onto this after all."

I gave my hand a jerk, but Mark held on tight. "This is not funny, Mark," I said. "Let go."

"Excuse me, did I hear you say Calloway?" a voice behind me suddenly asked.

For one split second, every single cell in my body simply froze. I barely even noticed that Mark London let go of my hand. Slowly I turned to face the person who'd spoken. That voice I'd have recognized anywhere.

"That's right," I said, pleased when my own voice came out clearly and steadily. "I'm Claire Calloway. I'm here from the Royer paper for the journalism exchange."

"Welcome to Beacon, Claire."

I looked up at him then. I could see his eyes widen in surprise as he took in my face, but it didn't stop him from extending his hand. A thing he'd done once before. The day we'd first met. The day I'd fallen in love with him.

"I'm student body president Alex Crawford."

Sixteen

You may as well stop wondering how I made it through the next few minutes. I can explain it in four words.

I do not know.

To this day it's all some bizarre and slightly painful blur, like swimming in a heavily chlorinated pool with your eyes open but without your goggles.

I'm pretty sure the obvious must have happened. I introduced Mark to Alex, and Alex to Mark. Then, promising to meet me in front of the school later that afternoon, Mark headed back to Royer. I have a vague recollection of him gunning the engine and of tires squealing as he pulled out of the parking lot. But by then I was well on my way to being in the grip of déjà vu. Once again I was arriving at Beacon as a "new" student, and Alex was showing me around.

The weekly student council meeting would be our first stop, Alex informed me as we made our way through campus gathering more than our fair share of stares as we went along. Though it could hardly be considered a part of every student's curriculum, the editor of the Beacon paper had thought the council meeting might be an event that I would like to cover.

The purpose of the meeting was to consider the various memorials proposed for recently deceased Beacon student Jo O'Connor.

"Before the meeting starts, there's something I think you should know, Claire," Alex said as we approached the classroom where, unbeknownst to Alex, I knew perfectly well the student council meetings were always held. He hesitated a moment, as if uncertain how to continue.

He's trying to figure out how to tell me I look just like his dead almost-girlfriend, I thought.

"You may have noticed we got some

strange looks as we came across campus," Alex went on.

"Yes, I did. Look, Alex," I said quickly. His name felt strange inside my mouth. "In all fairness, I think you should know that I'm aware that I . . . somewhat resemble Jo O'Connor. My editor at Royer pointed it out.

"I'm hoping nobody here will find the fact that I look like Jo too disturbing. I don't want to make anyone more upset than they already are. And I . . ."

Just say it, I thought.

"I know the two of you were close. Before we go any further, I want to say I'm sorry for your loss."

"Thank you," Alex said simply. "And I'm glad you already know. I was trying to figure out how to break it to you gently, I admit."

He gave me a somewhat ragged smile.

All of a sudden I felt like a total creep. I probably would have come clean right then and there if it hadn't been for the fact that doing so would have endangered my father.

"Thanks for being so nice about it," I

said. At this, Alex seemed to relax. He actually gave a chuckle.

"It's not as if you can help it," he said. He opened the door to the student council room. "After you."

"It is now official," I declared. "I am no longer living in the Twilight Zone. I am way past that. I've moved on to the Outer Limits."

"The outer limits of what?" Elaine asked.

"When I get there, I'll let you know."

It was late Friday afternoon, the end of my first week back at Beacon. By prior arrangement the day before, Elaine and I had met after school. We were doing the grocery shopping. With my father confined to the apartment, a lot of extra errands that he had taken care of were now falling to me.

As if I needed my life to be any more complicated.

Though we'd deliberately selected a store between our two neighborhoods, I had my notebook out as Elaine and I marched up and down the aisles. You never knew who you'd run into. If anyone saw us together, I could always claim I was conducting an interview.

One more.

In the week I'd been back, I'd already conducted what felt like about six thousand. The number of people wanting to talk about Jo O'Connor, or, more specifically, her ghost, had been nothing short of astonishing.

Actually it was really starting to creep me out and depress me, all at the same time. People actually *wanted* there to be a ghost. As far as I could tell, the fact that she'd died and come back from the dead was the thing people found most interesting about Jo O'Connor.

And then there were the memorials. The list up for discussion at Monday morning's student council session had contained ten ideas. By unanimous vote, the council had approved every single one of them.

One of the seats in the Little Theater already bore a plaque with my name. The botany club was busy with a Jo O'Connor Memorial Herb Garden, the centerpiece of which would be a letter J comprised entirely of rosemary plants.

Rosemary. That's for remembrance, in case you've forgotten. The reader board outside the school, which announced important activities for all to see, soon would bear my name. As would yet another plaque, this one at the base of the flagpole.

My favorite mid-morning treat at the snack bar, a chocolate donut and a Coke, was now called Jo's Special.

When I wasn't counting my blessings that no one had, as of yet, proposed to name one of the girls' bathrooms after me, or, even worse, one of the actual stalls, I was tearing my hair out over the fact that, in perpetuity throughout the universe, incoming senior chemistry students would be performing an experiment in my name. One involving chemicals that smelled just plain awful. Though I did appreciate the fact that my name wasn't attached to any of the biology dissections.

Yet.

"I just don't get it," I said as I tossed a bag of my favorite corn chips into the shopping cart. "So maybe I wasn't that high profile when I was a student here," I said. "But am I really more interesting dead than alive?"

"You don't seriously expect me to answer that, do you?" Elaine said.

"Yes. No. I don't know. I mean, don't get me wrong. I'm really touched that people want to remember me. It just all feels so unreal, somehow."

"Well, there is that part about Jo not really being dead."

"Elaine," I hissed. "Not so loud!"

"I just don't know what you're complaining about," Elaine hissed back.

"I'm not complaining," I said. I pulled open the cold case and added a carton of milk and a large container of low-fat raspberry yogurt to the cart. I was so upset, I almost shut the door on my hair.

"I'm just trying to say that none of the memorials feels like it's really about Jo O'Connor. I mean when she was alive. It's all about the ghost.

"Do you know why they're putting a bench in the herb garden? So Jo's ghost will have a congenial place to sit when she visits the campus. Suzy Neptune actually said that, right out loud."

"I admit that is a little weird," Elaine said.

"You're not kidding. But you know the weirdest thing of all?"

"No, but I have a feeling I'm about to be enlightened."

"Alex. Alex is the weirdest thing of all," I said. I leaned against an entire rack devoted to who knows how many different kinds of tortillas, and expelled a breath I hadn't even been aware I was holding in. "I can't believe I just said that. But it's absolutely true. He talks about her all the time."

"Why shouldn't he talk about her?" Elaine asked, and I could tell by her tone that she was upset. "Jo was important to Alex, in case you've forgotten."

"Of course I haven't forgotten," I said. "But Alex is just like everybody else, only more so. He doesn't talk about Jo O'Connor, living, breathing human being. Okay, formerly. He talks about her *ghost*. Doesn't that seem just the slightest bit odd to you? Does it sound like the Alex you know?"

"Under ordinary circumstances, no," Elaine said as we headed for the checkout line. "But the present circumstances are far from ordinary, you have to admit. Alex is probably coping the only way he can. I think it's hypocritical and selfish of you to criticize him for it, particularly as it's all your fault."

"What do you mean, it's all my fault?" I said.

"Well, you're the one who showed up dead in the first place."

"And *you're* the one who agreed with him when he said he'd seen a ghost. How come it's not *your* fault?"

"I didn't start this," Elaine said.

"Well, for your information, neither did I. What, exactly, do you think I did when my dad told me we had to fake our own deaths? Jump up and down and say, gee, Dad, that sounds like tons of fun?"

"Of course not," Elaine said quietly. "I just don't see why you had to come back, that's all."

"That's a horrible thing to say," I said.

We reached the checkout stand. In appalled silence, I piled my selections onto the belt, paid for the purchases, then snatched up the bag and headed for the door. Elaine trailed after, waiting until we were clear of the store before she spoke again.

"Jo . . . Claire." She stomped her foot with a cry of frustration. "Whatever your name is, stop where you are."

"I thought you'd be glad to see me," I said as I swung around to face her, horrified to feel tears behind my eyes. "I thought you'd be glad we could be friends again!"

"I don't mean *now*," Elaine said. "I mean *then*. Why did you have to come back then?" Without warning, she threw up her hands in disgust. "Oh, this is ridiculous. I can't even get straight what we're arguing about."

"That makes two of us," I said.

We stood for a moment in the parking lot, the grocery bag growing heavy on my hip.

"Of course I'm glad to see you," Elaine finally said. "But not this way. It feels . . . dishonest."

"You're right. You're absolutely right," I said. "I shouldn't have gotten angry. I'm sorry."

"God, I hate it when you do that," Elaine said.

"Do what?"

"Tell me I'm right before I have the chance to trounce you during the course of the argument."

We looked at each other for a moment.

"I should probably head for the bus stop," I said.

"Okay," Elaine said. She fell in step beside me. "Where's your usual ride? What's up with that guy, by the way? What's his name again?"

"Mark," I said. "Mark London. He's the Royer paper's star reporter. He was the one who was supposed to do this whole exchange in the first place, until everybody got all excited about how much Claire Calloway looked like Jo O'Connor."

"I'd keep your eye on him, if I were you," Elaine warned. "He looks at you all the time. As if he's waiting for something."

"Probably for me to screw up."

"I don't think so," Elaine said thoughtfully. "Or, at least, not entirely."

"Could you be more cryptic?" I inquired.

Elaine smiled.

"Actually, he probably *is* watching me,"

I said glumly. "While I'm over here having the exchange experience, he's back at Royer doing background research on Jo O'Connor."

"Uh-oh."

"You're not kidding," I said. "To tell you the truth, it's actually sort of a relief when he comes to pick me up. At least I know where he is. I'm starting to feel as if I spend every waking moment waiting for the other shoe to drop. I don't think I've felt so out of control in my entire life."

"Which life?"

"I'm thinking that would be my point."

"Does your dad know about the whole being-sent-back-to-Beacon thing?"

I shook my head.

"I just don't know how to tell him," I said. "I honestly think he'd freak if he knew, and Detective Mortensen would have a heart attack. If I can keep a low profile for the next couple of weeks, the exchange will be over and things will get back to normal. Or as close to normal as things can get until after the trial is over."

"What happens then?" Elaine asked.

"I don't know. Dad and I haven't even

talked about it. He's definitely sending out the don't-ask-questions vibe. Actually, I'm kind of worried about him."

"It'll be all right," Elaine consoled. "Isn't that what you said?"

"In a moment of insanity," I acknowledged.

Elaine reached over and gave my shoulders a quick squeeze. "Think positive," she said.

"Thanks," I said. "I'll do my best. What are you going to do this weekend?" I asked, trying to steer the conversation back to more normal channels.

Elaine hesitated.

"Actually, I'm going to spend some time with Alex. He said he just wanted to hang out, maybe catch a movie or something. I hope you don't mind."

"Why should I mind?" I asked. Though I did, of course. Elaine spending time with Alex because he was upset was one thing. Catching a movie sounded an awful lot like a date.

"I don't know. I just thought . . ." Elaine's voice trailed off.

"Unless you're trying to tell me I *should* mind."

"No, of course not. Don't be silly," Elaine said quickly.

"Because in that case I'd have to turn you into a ghost too."

"At least that would even the playing field," Elaine muttered.

I stopped. "What did you just say?" I asked.

"Nothing."

"It didn't sound like nothing to me."

"I was trying to reassure you," Elaine said, her voice just a little too loud. "There's no way Alex will even look at another girl as long as he thinks Jo's dead. Particularly not now that he's seen her ghost. So you don't have to worry about things like that."

"Why are you doing this?" I asked.

"Doing what?"

"Trying to make me feel even worse than I already do."

"I'm trying to make you feel *better*," Elaine protested.

"Well, it isn't working so knock it off!"

"You know what? I'm leaving," Elaine said.

"Fine, you do that. Have a nice weekend."

"I intend to."

Whirling around, she moved off quickly down the street. My anger kept me going until my bus arrived. I stomped on, paid my fare, and found a seat in the very back. No sooner did I sit down, though, than all my angry energy deserted me. I deflated, like a balloon with an air leak.

Great job, Calloway/O'Connor, I thought. *Alienate your one and only friend.*

Things were definitely getting way out of hand. With so many events out of my control, what chance did I have of making things right again?

That night I had a dream.

In it, I was being haunted by myself.

As is often the case, even with nightmares, the details of my dream were grounded in reality. I went shopping for my prom dress. Posters for prom had recently begun to decorate both the Royer and Beacon walls. Girls were whispering in corners. Guys were looking hunted. Big Date fever was in the air.

What could be more natural than that I'd dream of shopping for the perfect prom dress?

What could be more *un*natural than dreaming I was doing it at the Jo O'Connor Memorial Shopping Mall?

In order to get there, I'd taken Jo O'Connor Drive.

Even the vehicle I was piloting was dedicated to me. You know how sometimes you see those big SUVs with somebody's actual name on the back? That's what I was driving.

It was when I went to order that Seattle standard, a double tall latte, and the barrista asked me if I wanted to take home a pound of their new Jo O'Connor blend that I woke up. I jerked myself awake, heart pounding as if I'd just taken that pound of coffee and eaten it like it was a bowl of cornflakes.

This has got to stop. I've got to do something, I thought.

I had get rid of Jo O'Connor's ghost.

Seventeen

"Hey, Calloway. Check this out."

Mark London set a stack of books on my desk with a thump. It was the following Friday morning. A second excruciating week of the exchange had gone by.

On the one hand, I could congratulate myself on the fact that no new crises had occurred, though things between Elaine and me were still a little awkward. There'd also been no new proposals for Jo O'Connor memorials. On the other hand, I still hadn't figured out the way to get rid of the ghost. Maybe I'd get lucky and ghostmania would die down on its own.

Actually, during the second week of the

exchange, the biggest thorn in my side had been Mark London. He'd insisted on picking me up at lunch every day. And every single day he'd shared some new background tidbit on Jo O'Connor.

The irony of this did not escape me, by the way. As far as I could tell, the only person genuinely interested in who Jo had been when she was alive was the last person I wanted to know about her.

"These," I corrected now as I pushed my hair back over my shoulder. I regarded the stack of books Mark had just deposited on my desk with what I sincerely hoped was something other than a look of extreme alarm.

"*This* is singular. *These* is plural, a term which means more than one. You're never going to succeed as a journalist if you can't keep the basics straight."

He gave me a cheeky grin. "I love it when you get snotty," he said. "Now guess what those are."

"I don't have to guess," I said calmly, though my stomach was flopping like a fish out of water. "I know what they are. Yearbooks. This may come as a surprise to you, but I have actually seen them before."

"Not these, you haven't," he said.

That's what you think, I thought. Unless I was very much mistaken, the pile currently resting on my desk represented all the high schools attended by Jo O'Connor before she'd met her unfortunate demise.

Mark pulled up a chair and sat down beside me, sliding the top yearbook off the pile.

"This," he said. "Check *this* out." Quickly he flipped through the pages until he came to the freshman class pictures. "There," he said, stabbing his finger down against the page. "Right there."

I looked, my brow wrinkling. "You want me to look at a picture of William O'Brien?"

"Don't be dense, Calloway," Mark said. "She should be next, only she isn't."

"Where who should be?"

"Jo O'Connor. There's no freshman picture of her. Not in either of the yearbooks for the schools she attended freshman year. And there's none for sophomore year either."

Briskly he pulled another yearbook from the stack and performed the same demonstration. This time he pointed to a picture of Paul O'Dell. A couple of books later, there were no O' names at all. The pictures went right from Lyla Obritsch to Daniel Oda.

Not pictured, the listing read. Jo O'Connor.

"It's like she doesn't exist," Mark said. "Like she never existed."

"Of course she existed," I said. "She *died*. You pretty much have to exist before you can do that."

"Okay, well, how about this?" Mark said. He pulled a manila envelope from his backpack and slapped it on the desk beside the yearbooks. "She isn't in any grade school class pictures either."

"What?" This was a thing not even I had realized. "You mean none at all?"

"Not a single solitary one," Mark said. "Though, given the number of schools she attended, I suppose that's not surprising. The point I'm trying to make here is this: There is absolutely no photo documentation of Jo O'Connor. What if there's something really weird going on here? There's no way to verify that the Jo O'Connor pictured in the Beacon paper really *is* her. What if she's not the one who died?"

"That's the most ridiculous thing I've ever heard," I said. "I'd make an appointment with the school counselor to have that conspiracy theory problem checked, if I were you. Maybe there's a designer drug for it."

"Claire," Mr. Hanlon's voice's interrupted.

I jumped, then sucked in a deep breath. *Easy, girl,* I thought. Mark was on the wrong track. But the fact that his mind had leaped right to the conclusion that something wasn't quite right was still unsettling.

"I'm sorry, Mr. Hanlon. I didn't see you," I said.

He smiled. "And I'm sorry to interrupt. I just wanted you to know I think you've done an excellent job on these rough drafts. I particularly like your take on why so many students seemed to fixate so quickly on the possibility that there could even *be* a ghost."

"What's your theory?" Mark asked at once.

"That believing in a ghost helps ease the transition," I said.

"In what way?"

"Well, at first glance, the possibility of a ghost may seem farfetched," I said. "But believing in something that seems impossible, or at least unlikely, may actually be easier in the short run than accepting the truth: that someone you know has suffered a tragic accident."

Mark considered for a moment. "Okay," he said. "I'll buy that."

"That's a relief," I said.

"Keep up the good work," Mr. Hanlon said as he handed me back my drafts. I was pretty sure he was holding back a smile. "I pencilled in my comments. I look forward to reading the rest."

"Thanks again, Mr. Hanlon," I said.

He ambled away, leaving Mark and me alone.

"I have a ghost theory too," Mark London suddenly said. "You wanna hear it?"

"Do I have a choice?"

He gestured to the yearbooks, the envelope filled with grade school class pictures, all with a blank spot where Jo O'Connor should be.

"Jo O'Connor didn't have to die to become a ghost," Mark London said. "She's been one her whole life."

That night I dreamed again.

This time I knew it was a nightmare, right from the start. Everything was dim and foggy, like those scenes in a horror film when the heroine decides that, even though no girl with an ounce of sense would wander around in a graveyard at night, she's going to be overcome by an attack of the stupids and do it anyway.

In my dream I'm standing on a sidewalk. Fog obscures my feet, just like it always seems to obscure the ground in the movie graveyard, disguising unseen pitfalls. I don't quite know how I got to where I am, and for sure I don't know how I'd get away if I suddenly decided I needed to run. For just a moment, the fog obscures my vision too. Then it begins to clear and I can see what it is I'm standing in front of.

It's a school. Made of brick, tall and imposing. As I watch, students begin to rush toward it. I can hear shouts of joy as they recognize and greet one another.

Then, suddenly, I'm in the scene itself, and the students are all around me. Their momentum carries me up the steps to the school, then inside it. Abruptly, in one of those strange time-shifts that sometimes occur in dreams, I'm standing outside a classroom without ever having walked down the hallway. I'm clutching a school schedule in my hand.

This is where I'm supposed to be, I think in my dream. *Room 103.*

I open the door and go in. I find a seat in the back of the classroom and slide into it. From her desk at the head of the room, the teacher begins to call the roll. One by one, the students respond and raise their hands. I wait for my turn, tense and nervous. Identifying yourself as the new kid for the very first time is always hard, even if you've done it over and over.

"Jo O'Connor," the teacher calls out.

I raise my hand. "Here," I reply.

The teacher's brow furrows in some emotion I can't quite identify. Confusion. Annoyance. A combination of both. She gazes around the classroom, her glance sweeping like a searchlight.

"Jo O'Connor," she calls once more, a little louder.

I raise my hand a little higher, waggling it in the air. *"Here!"* I cry.

This time I can tell the teacher is annoyed. She makes a mark in red pen beside my name in the roll book, shaking her head back and forth. At this, I actually get to my feet.

"Here! I'm Jo O'Connor, and I'm right here," I call.

Not one student turns her or his head. It's as if I don't exist, as if I'm not there at all.

Now the time in the dream seriously speeds up, like watching a video on fast-forward. Only in the movie that's suddenly become my life, it's the same scene playing over and over. I sit in the back of classroom after classroom as roll is called. Each and every time the teacher comes to my name, I respond and raise my hand. Each and every time, not one person notices.

Finally I can't take it anymore. Hurling myself out of my seat, I run from the classroom and dash down the hall. I run straight to the nearest girls' bathroom.

There, heart pounding, staring into the mirror above the sinks, I discover the terrible truth.

I no longer exist. I've succeeded so well in blending in that I've erased myself entirely. Not even I can see myself.

I woke up with Mark London's voice ringing in my ears. *I think Jo O'Connor's been a ghost her whole life.*

No, I thought. *It isn't true. You weren't there. You don't know how it was.*

But no matter what I did, I couldn't seem to convince myself. Not entirely anyhow. All I could think of was that old riddle about a tree falling in a forest. If there's no one to hear it, does its falling still make a sound?

If the only proof of her existence lay in Jo O'Connor's heart, a thing she'd never really shared with anyone, who was to say she'd ever existed at all?

Eighteen

"I can't believe you talked me into this," Elaine said.

"I didn't talk you into it. You volunteered."

"Only because I knew you'd do it without me if I didn't go along."

"I have to do this. It's the only way," I said.

It was Monday morning and we were in the Little Theater, right before Drama class. Somewhere in the wee hours of the morning following my conversation with Mark London followed by my nightmare, I'd finally figured out what I had to do. The way to lay Jo O'Connor's ghost to rest.

Paradoxically, I'd decided it wasn't to finish her off, as I'd originally envisioned.

It was to bring her back for one last appearance instead.

Along about four a.m., I'd come to the inescapable conclusion that the only way for Jo's ghost to fade away was to have her show up again. She could talk to Alex, tell him how much she appreciated everything he was doing for her, but relate how all the memorials in her honor were keeping her tied to the mortal plane. A thing that wasn't healthy for anyone.

The trick was making sure Alex was in the right place at the right time for the ghostly manifestation to occur. And making sure he was alone. Arranging this was something I didn't feel I could do all on my own, so I'd enlisted Elaine's reluctant help. Extremely reluctant help.

"Are you out of your mind?" she'd all but yelled early that morning when I'd put our secret contact plan to work and managed to reach her on the phone. "That's insane. It'll never work. It's a terrible idea. In fact, it may be the worst idea I've ever heard."

"Stop exaggerating," I'd said into the phone. "I've been thinking about this all night, Elaine. I can't be just a ghost. There's got to be more to me than that."

I could feel my voice rising hysterically.

"Of course there's more to you than being a ghost," Elaine said, her own voice calming. "Who put that ridiculous idea into your head?"

"Mark London," I confessed.

Elaine gave a snort. "I knew that guy was bad news," she said. "I wouldn't take any action based on his opinion, if I were you."

"Look, Elaine. I really have thought about this all night," I said. "This obsession with Jo's ghost has got to stop. She's the only one who can make that happen, but she can't do it on her own. She needs your help. *I* need your help. Please don't let me—us—down."

"That was an extremely low blow," Elaine said. "And stop talking about yourself as if you're more than one person. You're creeping me out."

"I am more than one person," I said. "And they both have the same question: Was that a yes or a no?"

Elaine was silent for a moment. "Yes, I will help. No, I won't let you down," she finally said. "But I want to go on record as officially saying I think this idea completely bites and you'll live to regret it."

"Look on the bright side, then," I said. "You'll get to say I told you so. Okay, here's what I need you to do. . . ."

A few sentences later the plan was in place. Elaine would ask Alex to meet her in the Little Theater before Drama. It would actually be easier for them to be alone than it sounds. The Beacon schedule called for this sort of mini-break to occur between second and third periods. Students got an extra fifteen minutes. Most used the break to grab a mid-morning snack before ambling along to the next class.

When a deplorable tendency toward lateness for third period had developed, the school authorities had threatened to cancel the break entirely. This had resulted in to-the-minute promptness. In fact, it had become something of a schoolwide contest to see who could cut it the closest and still officially be on time. It was a pretty safe bet that no one would be heading to the Little Theater early.

Even Mr. Barnes would be assisting the plan, although he didn't know it. Like clockwork, he used the break to go for a quick latte. He'd be out of the building for those fifteen minutes. The combination of circumstances wouldn't buy me a lot of time, it was true, but I was hoping it would be enough to convince Alex it was time to let Jo O'Connor go.

"How do I look?" I asked Elaine now.

She studied me for a moment. "Like a cross between a cat burglar and a Kabuki performer," she said. "Without the white makeup."

"That's very helpful. Thanks so much," I said.

Since there wasn't a lot of time to put my plan into action, I'd decided to make use of Claire Calloway's fashion sense to help Jo's ghost show up. The theory was that I, Jo, would materialize from between the black masking curtains that hung at the back of the stage. To that end, I hadn't changed my clothes, but I had tucked Claire's long hair up inside a black nylon stocking.

The idea was to get Alex to focus on the most recognizable thing about me: my face. Elaine had already made a quick trip to the light booth to supply suitable ghostly illumination. The auditorium lights were off. Only the lights at the back of the stage were on, down low.

I'd make my appearance, plead with Alex to let me move on, then disappear with a little more lighting help from Elaine. If that didn't work, I wasn't quite sure what I'd do.

Don't think like that. Think positive, I thought. *This is going to work. It's got to.*

"Okay, I think I'm set," I said. "You'd better get up to the booth. Alex should be here any minute."

"All right," Elaine said. She turned to go, her expression stony. I knew that look. It's the look Elaine's face gets when she's really upset about something and either can't or won't talk about it.

"Elaine," I said.

She turned back. "What?"

"I know you don't want to do this, but you're doing it anyway. So I just want to say, thanks."

Her expression softened. "You're welcome. Just remember, you owe me one."

"As if you'd let me forget."

A quick smile flitted across Elaine's features as she turned toward the booth once more.

"Elaine? Are you there?" we suddenly heard a voice call out.

For one split second both Elaine and I froze. "Omigod. That's Alex," I said. "Get up to the booth. Hurry. Go."

Elaine sprinted up a side aisle toward the tech booth while I dashed to the back of the stage. I'd just made it behind the curtains when I heard Alex's voice once more.

"Elaine?"

All of a sudden I could hear the stage lights start to make the funny humming sound that sometimes happens when the levels change. I knew Elaine had made it safely to the booth. From there she'd literally set the stage. The rest was up to me.

"Alex," I moaned. "Aleeex."

"Elaine, what's going on? Where are you?" Alex asked. "And by the way, that isn't very funny."

Great, I thought. My less-than-sterling

impersonation of my own ghost had so far succeeded only in making Alex annoyed. If I couldn't do better than that, I'd really be sunk.

I pulled in a deep breath to steady my nerves.

"I'm not Elaine," I said in my own voice.

"What's going on?" Alex said.

I eased my head out from between the curtains, sincerely hoping I looked like a face floating in the air. I could just make out Alex's form. He was standing in front of the first row of seats, gazing up at the stage. I knew the moment he saw me. He sucked in an audible breath.

"*Jo!*"

He put his hands flat on the stage as if to hoist himself up.

"Don't come any closer, Alex!" I said. "I won't be able to stay if you do."

Slowly Alex dropped back down. "Jo, is that really you?" he asked.

"It's really me, Alex," I said. "I don't have much time, but we have to talk. I had to see you. There's something I have to try to make you understand."

"*Understand?*" Alex said. "I don't *understand* any of this. How can this be happening? How can you be here at all? I mean . . . I thought that you were . . ." His voice trailed off.

He doesn't want to say it, I thought. *He doesn't want to say the word "dead."*

"That's why I'm here. To explain," I said. In his confusion, Alex had given me precisely the opening I'd wanted. If I could convince him the reason I was still around was because he hadn't let me move on . . .

"Alex, I know you . . . care about me," I began. "But you've got to listen. You've got to let . . ."

"Oh, Jo! I knew I wasn't making it up or hallucinating. I knew you'd really come back," Alex burst out suddenly. "I knew you'd give me the chance to explain."

"Explain what?" I asked, the question out before I could stop it. "Alex, what are you talking about?"

"It was . . . that after . . . ," Alex said, "before the accident, when I asked you to go to the prom. I kissed you."

"I remember," I said.

All of a sudden a horrible suspicion

began to dawn. If we'd had a conversation like this under other, less otherworldly circumstances, I'd have pretty much had to figure that . . .

"Alex Crawford, are you trying to tell me you *take it back?*"

At my words, relief flooded Alex's face. *I don't believe this!* I thought.

"Oh, god, Jo. I'm sorry. I'm so sorry," Alex said. "I tried my best to make it up to you. I got the student council to approve all those memorials."

"You do mean it," I said. "This is unbelievable. You're taking it back. I haven't even been dead a month and you're telling me you never really liked me in the first place. What happened to love at first sight?"

"Omigod!" a girl's voice I couldn't identify screeched. "There she is! There's Jo O'Connor's ghost! I think she and Alex are having a fight!"

Alex's whole body jerked. His head whipped around like a sports fish on a line. I could hear my heartbeats, those things I was no longer supposed to have, thundering like a jackhammer in my ears. Though it could have just been the sound of all those footsteps suddenly pounding down the theater aisles.

I had no idea how many of them there were.

I didn't particularly want to stop to count.

"Hey, Jo, what's it feel like to be dead?" I heard a guy call.

I did the only thing I could. I answered the question.

"Right at this moment, it pretty much sucks eggs," I said.

Then, finally, Elaine killed the lights, plunging the auditorium into total darkness.

During the confusion which ensued, I was the only one who kept my head. I whipped it back behind the curtains, yanked the stocking cap off my hair, and ran. Out the side stage door, down the short flight of steps, straight into Mr. Barnes.

"For heaven's sake!" he exclaimed. "What is it? You look like you've just seen—"

"Oh, Mr. Barnes," I sobbed out. "I've just seen the ghost of Jo O'Connor."

Nineteen

"The minute I stepped into that theater, I *knew*. I just *knew* there was something freaky going on. I mean, I'm not even *in* Drama. How did I know to even go there in the first place? But then, all the women in my family are like that."

I paused in the act of doodling instead of taking interview notes and glanced across the table at Khandi Kayne.

"Like what?" I inquired.

Several hours and what felt like several hundred interviews later, I was sitting in the library study carrel I'd established as my private office. It had a number of advantages. I could close the door, giving those students who came to see me a certain amount of privacy.

Spending the entire day at Beacon was a break in the routine. Following my encounter with Mr. Barnes, I'd phoned Mr. Hanlon and informed him of the latest ghost sighting. I figured it would look a little weird if I didn't. He'd given his permission for me to remain at Beacon for the day, interviewing as many people as possible.

I could have done without Khandi Kayne.

"We *know* things," Khandi said now, dropping her voice to a conspiratorial whisper. "The women in my family, I mean. We can just sense them."

I drew a little witch's hat with an arrow poking through the crown.

"You mean supernatural things?"

She nodded. "Personally I wasn't one bit surprised to walk into that theater and see Jo O'Connor's ghost. I knew as soon as I put my hand on the door handle that something funny was going on. I got all sort of lightheaded."

Probably the blood trying to find its way through the labyrinth of your brain.

"I think it was because I could sense something evil," Khandi went on.

Oh boy, I thought. *Here we go.*

Khandi had wanted to stab me, stab Jo O'Connor, in the back from the day we'd first met. Who says delayed gratification can't be fun?

"So, let me get this straight," I said. "You're saying Jo O'Connor's ghost is evil?"

"Well, maybe not actually evil. That might be too strong a word," Khandi said. "But did you ever hear of a happy ghost haunting someone? I just don't think that happens. Besides, Jo wasn't very good for Alex when she was alive. Why should she be good for him now that she's dead?"

"It sounds as if you didn't like her very much," I commented.

Khandi gave a trill of nervous laughter as she eyed my notebook. "Well, I don't know that I'd go that far," she said. "I mean, I'd hate for you to quote me or anything. It's just . . . I never really felt Jo was right for Alex. She only wanted to go out with him because he was student body president."

You are so *full of it,* I thought. Images of red and white Christmas candy canes danced through my brain. I seized them and snapped their little striped necks. I flipped through my notebook, pretending to look for previously recorded information.

"I understand he asked her to the prom."

"I wouldn't know anything about that," Khandi said with a sniff. "But I'll tell you this." She leaned forward as if about to impart a great secret.

"If Alex did ask her, it was because he felt sorry for her. But it totally backfired on him. I think that's why Jo's ghost is still here. She just can't bear to let Alex go. Even she knows she's a nobody without him."

Nobly, I resisted the impulse to stuff my notebook down her throat.

"That's an . . . interesting insight," I said.

"Oh, well," Khandi said, sitting back and preening ever so slightly. "All the women in my family are like that."

"They know things and they have insights. Fascinating combination."

"We like to think so," Khandi said.

The bell rang, saving me from further information on the matriarchs of the Kayne clan.

"Thanks a lot for your time," I said, closing my notebook to signal that the interview was over.

"Don't you want a picture of me?" Khandi asked.

By the end of the day I'd compiled the following fascinating facts. Jo O'Connor's ghost had:

1) Confronted Alex in the Little Theater, vowing to haunt him forever over the fact that he intended to dump her. (I probably don't have to tell you that one came from Khandi. Ironically it was the only one that came anywhere near being accurate.)

2) Been seen sitting at her favorite table in the snack bar eating a chocolate donut and drinking a Coke during morning break.

3) Appeared on the basketball court

in the middle of senior boys' P.E. A thing which had caused the school's best free throw shot maker to miss the basket. A circumstance which he insisted would otherwise never have occurred, it was so unusual.

4) Shown up in the office of Ms. Geyer, the head school counselor, pleading with her to be allowed to attend graduation. Ms. Geyer was briefly treated for hypertension, then sent home for the rest of the day.

And those were just my top four faves.

As far as I could tell, about the only people on campus *not* claiming to have seen Jo O'Connor's ghost were the two who might legitimately be able to say they'd actually done so: Alex and Elaine. Both had kept their distance throughout the day. Elaine had gotten her two cents in, however. Stuffed into the locker assigned to Claire Calloway was a note that said, "I told you so."

"Claire?"

I jumped, the pen I clutched in my

numb fingers making a jagged line across the notebook page. All day long I'd waited for this moment with a mixture of dread and anticipation.

"Hey, Alex," I said.

He looked absolutely awful. Tired and drained. *He looks confused and unhappy,* I thought, and felt guilt swarm up to choke me.

"Okay if I sit down?" Alex asked.

"Sure," I said.

Alex pulled out a chair and sat down across from me. I made sure my glasses were securely on my face.

Don't think about Jo O'Connor now, I thought. *Don't think about all the mistakes you've made. Concentrate on being Claire Calloway. On doing her—your—job.*

"I wanted to thank you," Alex said.

I felt my jaw wobble as I struggled not to let it drop open.

"That's nice. What for?" I asked.

A faint smile moved across Alex's tired face.

"For not immediately hounding me with billions of questions I don't know how to answer."

"Oh, that," I said. I flipped open the notebook to a clean page. "So, Alex, how was your day?" I asked.

He laughed, and I could feel some of the tension flow out of him.

"I think the safest thing I can say is *interesting*," he said. "I was wondering if I could . . . talk to you about it."

"That's what I'm here for," I said, wishing my heart wasn't beating quite so fast. "Where would you like to start?"

"I don't quite know."

"How about if I ask questions, then?" I said. "I think that's why they call this an interview."

Alex smiled again.

"So, tell me. Do you usually play things safe?"

Alex looked surprised. "What makes you ask that?"

"The phrase you just used," I answered. "You said, 'the safest thing I can say'. Somehow, it made me wonder whether the choices you're used to making are the safe ones. It's always seemed unusual to me that someone with your track record would see a ghost at all."

Who are you? I thought. *Will you tell me, Alex?*

"Okay," he said. "I guess I get that. And the answer would have to be yes. I think that was one of the things that first attracted me to Jo."

"What do you mean?" I asked.

"Jo was different," Alex said.

"It seems that you and"—I made a show of consulting my notebook— "Khandice Kayne would agree on that."

Alex snorted. "Don't even go there," he said.

"Is it true what they say?"

"Depends what it is."

"That you fell head over heels for Jo O'Connor, then realized you'd made a mistake. It's been suggested you were going to dump her, but she died before you got the chance. I'm sorry if that sounds unfeeling."

"I was *not* going to dump her," Alex said, his tone emphatic. "You can't dump someone unless you've actually gone out."

"I think you're playing with semantics," I said. "The impression I've gotten over the last couple of weeks is that you and Jo were attracted right from the start.

Today people are saying her ghost totally freaked because you told her you'd made a mistake. That's kind of confusing, don't you agree?"

Alex was silent, staring down at the tabletop. On impulse, I closed the notebook with a snap.

"Totally off the record," I said. "I won't use anything you tell me in an article unless you give me permission. What was really going on between you and Jo O'Connor?"

Just tell me the truth. Whatever it is.

Alex gave a sigh. "Do you believe in love at first sight?" he asked.

"Maybe," I answered.

His eyes flickered to my face, understanding in them. "Before I met Jo, that's exactly what I would have said. But there was something about her that struck me right off. She was . . ."

"Different," I filled in, using the word he'd used just a few moments ago.

"That's right," Alex said. "The first time I saw her, she was standing at that burger joint across the street. You know the one?"

I nodded.

"Staring at something that wasn't there."

"That *is* different, I have to admit."

At this, he actually gave a rueful laugh.

He feels better talking about it, I thought. I wondered how I'd feel by the interview's end.

"I think that made more sense inside my head. What I mean to say is that she looked interested. As if she was trying to figure out a puzzle and was willing to stand there until she did. Most people would have walked right on by and never noticed anything was unusual. Or they would have pretended not to notice even if they had. Jo wasn't like that. She didn't seem to be afraid of what other people thought."

"Surely everybody's afraid of that, to a certain degree," I countered.

"Okay," Alex nodded. "I'll give you that. But Jo never came across that way. If anything, it was just the opposite. It was almost as if it didn't occur to her to worry about what other people thought because she knew what they were thinking before they did."

Boy, did you give Jo the benefit of the doubt, I thought.

"So you're saying she was psychic," I couldn't resist saying, deadpan.

Alex gave a quick, surprised laugh. Then, slowly, his smile faded as he considered. "I think what I'm saying is that she understood how people fit together," he said. "She had a perspective nobody else had. Totally without realizing it, she made *me* see how much of my life was same old, same old."

"But you thought you made a mistake," I said.

"About being in love with her. Not about her being great," Alex said. "I just suddenly realized she wasn't the one I wanted."

"Who do you want, Alex?" I asked.

Alex shook his head swiftly, and I felt a sharp emotion shoot through my chest. Relief. Disappointment. What I was doing really wasn't fair.

"Even off the record, I can't tell you that. It wouldn't make a difference anyway. She doesn't know. I didn't want to say anything until I'd talked to Jo, and then . . ."

"Then Jo was kind of hard to talk to," I filled in. "Is that what you were trying to do today? Tell her the truth at last?"

"Sort of," Alex said. "You probably think I'm nuts for thinking I see her ghost at all, don't you?"

"Oh, I don't know," I said. "It's better not to rule out too many possibilities, in my experience."

"Now you sound just like her," he said.

I swallowed past a lump in my throat that was easily the size of the state of Texas.

"Does this mean you'll let me give some advice?" I asked.

"Just so long as it's not take two aspirin and call me in the morning."

"Do you think Jo would want you to be unhappy?"

"That's your advice?"

"It's a question and I think you should answer it," I said. "Is—was—Jo the sort of person who'd want you to move on, or would she want you to be all obsessed by guilt over what happened in the past?"

"People always do that, you know," Alex said.

"Do what?"

"Ask themselves what the person who's dead would have wanted. Personally, I think it's an excuse to go ahead and do what they want."

"Answer the question, Alex."

"I didn't want to hurt her," he burst out. "Everybody'd seen the way I felt. It's not like I tried to hide it. How was I going to explain I'd gotten it wrong? I just didn't know what to do."

On impulse, I reached out and covered his hand with mine.

"I get that," I said. "Maybe Jo does too. Maybe that's why she came back. To tell you that she understands. That she wants you to move on, to be happy. Maybe *she* can't move on until *you* do. Did you ever think of that?"

"No, I didn't," Alex admitted.

"Try thinking about it now," I said. "After what you've told me about her, it's hard for me to believe Jo would want you to walk around being miserable, though I bet she wouldn't mind if Khandi Kayne did."

Alex gave me a slow smile. "Okay, I'll think about it," he said.

"Good." I took my hand from his. My fingers tingled, just like they had when we'd clasped hands the very first day we'd met. Only now I had a feeling I knew the cause: Whatever had happened between Alex and me was over. We'd never hold hands again.

"It's getting kind of late. I'd better go," I said.

I stuffed my notebook into my bag and rose to my feet.

"Before you do, can I ask you a question?" Alex asked.

"Of course you can," I said.

"Will you go to the Beacon prom with me, Claire?"

Twenty

"What did you just say?" I asked, stupified.

Before Alex could respond, I held up a hand.

"Please excuse me. That sounded very rude, and I didn't mean for it to. It's just . . . you've kind of surprised me, I have to admit."

"That's my fault. I'm sorry," Alex said, his face beginning to turn red. "I just thought you might like someone to go with when you cover the event for the paper," he plowed on. "I think that's supposed to be part of the exchange, isn't it?"

"I honestly don't know, but I suppose it would make sense," I said. "Wouldn't that be kind of boring for you? I mean, it's not like it would be a real date. Right?"

"Right," Alex said. "But you would be doing me a favor. I'm pretty much expected to go. . . ."

"Why don't you ask what's her name?" I asked.

"What's her name?"

"I don't know. You wouldn't tell me," I said.

Alex expelled air as he got the lame joke I'd made.

"Look," I said. "I appreciate the gesture. I honestly do. But it's your one and only senior prom, Alex. Don't you think you should go with someone who means something to you instead of someone you barely know? If you won't ask the mystery girl of your dreams, why not ask Elaine Golden?"

"Elaine?" Alex echoed, his face stunned. "What made you suggest her?"

"Wasn't she Jo's closest friend? She'd be likely to understand if you wanted a date that wasn't really a date, wouldn't she?"

"I guess so. Maybe," Alex said.

"I'll tell you what. You ask Elaine, and the three of us can meet up ahead of time,"

I suggested. "It *would* be nice for me to have someone to walk in the door with. Then you and Elaine can party while I cover the event. How does that sound?"

"Okay. Actually, it sounds good," Alex said. All of a sudden he smiled, his blue eyes dancing. It was the first time all day I'd seen him look truly happy.

"You know, I put off coming to see you today. I was kind of dreading talking to you, as a matter of fact. I shouldn't have. You've made me feel a lot better."

"Thanks," I said. "Though I warn you, I will have to do an official interview for the paper one of these days."

"Okay," Alex said. "I'll let you know when I'm ready. Thanks, Claire."

"You're welcome, Alex," I said.

"Okay, so, I guess I'll see you around."

"I guess so," I said.

Alex moved to open the door of the study carrel. Before he could even get his hand on the knob, the door swung open to reveal Mark London.

"There you are," Mark said. "I've been looking all over for you. You're never going to believe what happened."

"There's been another ghost sighting. I know," I said. "Why do you think I've been here all day?"

Before I'd even finished speaking, Mark was shaking his head from side to side. "No, not that."

"Then what?" I asked.

"I think I know the answer," Alex said. "I would have mentioned it before, but I thought you knew."

I pulled in a give-me-patience breath.

"Knew what?" I asked.

"Jo O'Connor's been nominated for Prom Queen."

Mark made a derisive sound. "You mean her ghost has."

Twenty-one

"Second Ghost Sighting Prompts Dead Student's Nomination"

Ticket sales shoot through the roof as Beacon students ask themselves the question: Will Jo O'Connor's ghost attend the prom?

BY MARK LONDON,
SPECIAL TO THE ROYER REGISTER

Prom.

It needs no introduction. Its mystique requires no explanation. Though it's unlikely students today attend the same prom their parents did, the way they think about it may be more similar than the people involved might care to acknowledge.

Prom.

It's important. A necessary part of the end-of-high-school ritual. A night when magic happens. When anything is possible. And nowhere is this more apparent than at Beacon High School, where a student has been posthumously nominated for Prom Queen.

Of course, the fact that students all over campus claim to have seen her ghost doesn't hurt.

I refer, of course, to recently deceased Beacon student Jo O'Connor.

In the weeks following her tragic accidental death, multiple memorials have been both planned and implemented in O'Connor's honor. But none is more touching, and unusual, than the Prom Queen nomination, which came just hours after the most recent claims of a ghost sighting.

The fact that the nomination has spurred brisk ticket sales isn't surprising to prom organizers.

"People are excited and curious," acknowledged prom committee chair Theresa Aragon. "Who wouldn't be? Those are normal human emotions. Personally I hope Jo wins and her ghost shows up to wear the crown."

Strong words, particularly from someone who's been nominated for Prom Queen herself.

Will Jo O'Connor be elected Prom Queen? Will her ghost appear to claim the crown? Only time will tell. Regardless of the final outcome, Beacon students can already say one thing for sure: Their prom experience will most definitely be one of a kind.

"Will you look at that?" I said as I tossed the latest edition of the Royer school paper down on the coffee shop table with a slap. It was the day following my interview with Alex, the day following my most

recent ghost sighting. Though I was supposed to be covering events at Beacon for
the Royer paper, Mark London had scooped
me and dashed off a quick article about the
Beacon prom.

"Is that disgusting or what? Publicity.
Exactly what I do *not* want. Thank good-
ness Detective Mortensen doesn't have
time to read the school paper. At least, I
don't think he does. He's too busy getting
dad ready to testify. They're saying the trial
could start any time now. I hope it does, for
both our sakes. I'm getting a little tired of
Law and Order reruns."

Elaine made a consoling sound as she
took a sip of her favorite treat drink, a
double tall white chocolate mocha. She
allows herself this treat under only two
conditions: extreme stress or extreme
delight. I hadn't yet figured out what
today's reason was, but I had my hopes.

Unlike our other meetings lately, Elaine
had called this one. At her suggestion we'd
met after school in the Starbucks at the
Convention Center downtown, a thing
which dovetailed nicely with an errand Dad
wanted me to run.

"You've got whipped cream on your nose," I said.

"Alex asked me to the prom."

I felt a bubble of relief well up and burst inside my chest.

"Great," I responded with genuine enthusiasm. "At least one thing is going right."

"You're not mad?" Elaine asked as she dabbed her face with a napkin.

"Mad?" I echoed. "Of course not. Why should I be? It was my idea in the first place."

Elaine's hand paused in midair.

"What?"

"He asked me first," I said, so relieved I was totally oblivious to her reaction. "I mean, he asked Claire Calloway. It was right after the interview we did about the most recent sighting of Jo's ghost. He asked if I wanted to go to the prom, but I knew he really didn't mean it. He just wanted me to not feel funny about showing up to cover the event without an escort."

"And you suggested he take me instead," Elaine said softly. Slowly and carefully, she set the damp napkin back down on the table, then smoothed it out. I think it was the way she moved that finally got through to me. Precise and controlled. But I could see the way her fingers quivered, as if she was longing to bend them into fists.

"What's the matter?" she asked, her tone still quiet. "Didn't you think I could get a date on my own?"

"Of course I didn't think that," I protested. "I'll tell you the same thing I told Alex. That he ought to go to his senior prom with someone who meant something to him, not a complete stranger. Someone who'd understand . . ."

Appalled at what I'd been about to say, my voice petered out.

"Someone who'd understand that the invitation itself didn't really mean anything," Elaine filled in for me. "Someone who wouldn't even have to be told the evening didn't constitute a real date. A person who wouldn't mind that she was just a stand-in for Jo O'Connor."

"No," I said. "That isn't what I meant. Besides, Alex told me . . ."

"I don't care what he told you," Elaine cut me off. "Did you even stop for a minute to think about how this would make me feel? Or did you just assume I'd be happy to take your leftovers?"

That was the moment it hit me, right between the eyes. *How blind can one person be?* I thought.

"You're in love with him, aren't you?"

"Don't be ridiculous," Elaine choked out. "That would be a totally lost cause. Why would I waste my valuable time doing a stupid thing like that?"

"How does *because you can't help it* sound?"

"About right."

We stared at one another across the formica-topped table. "How long have you known?" I asked.

Elaine took a fortifying sip of mocha. "Try asking when I didn't know. I think it's a shorter period of time."

"You could have said something. How long have you guys known one another?

"Since kindergarten."

"Geez, Elaine," I exploded. "Why on earth didn't you *say* something? Tell me to back off?"

"What would have been the point?" Elaine asked. "It was obvious to everyone Alex was totally gone on you. Then you had to go and be all generally likeable. There wasn't much I could do after I realized that."

"I'm so sorry," I said.

"Yeah, well, you ought to be."

"Elaine," I said softly. "I—Jo—isn't the one Alex was gone over."

"Don't be ridiculous," Elaine began.

"No, I mean it," I said. "He told me so just yesterday afternoon."

"What?" Elaine exclaimed, her eyes widening.

"Alex gave Claire an interview today," I said. "Off the record. He talked about Jo O'Connor. He told me that the very night she died, he realized something completely unexpected: He was actually in love with someone else. That's part of the reason Alex has been so obsessed by the whole ghost thing. He feels guilty."

"I don't believe it," Elaine said.

"Are you calling me a liar?"

She shook her head as if rearranging her brain cells.

"Of course not," she said. "So, who's the lucky girl?"

"I don't know."

"Oh, come *on*," Elaine exclaimed. "He told you he was in love with someone else, and you didn't ask him who she was?"

"I asked," I said simply. "He wouldn't tell. He said she didn't know. He hadn't wanted to do anything until he'd tried to explain things to Jo. Unfortunately a fatal accident intervened before he could."

"That's the trouble with Alex," Elaine said after a moment. "He's a really nice guy."

"I'd have to second that," I said.

Elaine regarded me thoughtfully. "You don't seem all that upset."

"You know?" I said. "I'm not. I've been thinking about this a lot, and I have a theory about what happened with Alex and me. I do think we saw something in each other, just not what we thought.

"Alex kept saying I was different. That was the thing about me that attracted him right off. But what I liked about him was that he was so easily recognizable. Big Man on Campus, in the nicest way possible. He made me believe that I could fit, that I could belong. Boy, does that sound like I need therapy," I said as I put my head down in my hands.

"Maybe I'd better have one of those mochas."

"I'll buy you one," Elaine offered. "Jo, I mean Claire." She blew out an exasperated breath and I lifted my head. "God, I wish things were back to normal! What I'm trying to say is I realize I haven't been all that understanding lately. I want you to know I'm sorry."

"I'm sorry too," I said. "I know I've asked a lot of you and we don't really know each other all that well. That isn't what it feels like, though. It pretty much feels as if I've known you forever. I'd be a raving lunatic without you, for sure I know that much."

Elaine grimaced as tears filled her eyes. "Some friend you are. Trying to make me cry in public."

"Is it going to work?"

"No way."

"And another great Calloway/O'Connor plan bites the dust."

"Is this the moment where we vow never to let any guy come between us, no matter what?" Elaine asked.

"I think so. Elaine," I said. "What am I going to do? I can't see my way out."

Elaine reached to cover my hands with her own, her grip both strong and consoling. The same way I'd comforted Alex the day before.

"What every senior girl dreams of doing," she said. "We're going to the prom. With the student body president no less. Then we're going to watch him like hawks to see if we can figure out who he wishes he were taking instead of us."

"Do we have to wear twin dresses?"

Elaine laughed. All of a sudden, I realized I was grinning like an idiot.

"You wanna go shop?"

Twenty-two

In the movie version of my story, this is the scene where Elaine and I get all girly as we shop together. Or, as a variation, Alex may even be involved. In a wacky montage, Elaine and I try on a variety of personality-defying outfits, while some great song plays in the background.

Everything about this scene is happy. The lighting is warm and golden, even in a fluorescent-filled department store. The actors playing Alex, Elaine, and me display their expensive dental work throughout. Not only that, Alex is endlessly patient through the countless changes of clothing.

This is just one of the ways in which

you can tell it's a fantasy and not real life.

In reality, Elaine and I did eventually shop together. We did find dresses for the prom. They were not the same dress, and Alex did not go with us.

Duh.

But before any of that occurred, I had a close and confusing encounter with Mark London.

It happened right after my heart-to-heart with Elaine, in fact. She'd already departed for home. I waited fifteen minutes, then headed off for the safe apartment. This was a combination of the routine Elaine and I had developed so we didn't seem to be paling around too much, and what our individual bus schedules required.

Rather than just sitting by myself at the table, I decided I'd get a jump on searching for a prom dress by doing a little window shopping. I'd just gotten up from the table to carry out this plan when I heard a voice say:

"You certainly are getting chummy with Elaine Golden."

Though my heart was racing, I turned

around slowly. I didn't need to face him to know who it was.

"I might consider backing off if I were you," I said. "Otherwise I'll have to report you to Mr. Hanlon for stalking."

He snorted. "I'm a reporter," he said. "It's my job."

"What about the part where you're incredibly obnoxious? Is that in the job description too, or just a personality disorder?"

"You always come out swinging, don't you, Calloway?" Mark London said. "It kind of makes a guy wonder what you've got to hide."

"I think they call that blaming the victim," I came right back. "And for your information, it went out about twenty years ago."

I grabbed my bag and attempted to brush by him. He caught me by the arm. I stopped. We were shoulder to shoulder now. Eye to eye.

"You really want to let go of me," I said.

Just for a second, I was sure I saw the last thing I expected flare in his dark eyes.

"No, I don't," he said.

But he did it anyhow, stepping back, his expression shuttered now.

Run! my brain screamed. The rest of me stayed right where I was.

"You really think I'm her, don't you?" I heard myself say. "That's what this is really all about. You're not attracted to me, London. You just want to solve a puzzle. Prove you're the smartest."

"Yes. No. I don't know," Mark said. He made a disgusted sound and dragged a hand through his hair. "There are just too many coincidences for me. Combined with too many things that don't add up."

"Maybe I'm just a woman of mystery," I said.

He gave a sudden bark of laughter. "Maybe, but I doubt it. I'll say this, though. You're full of surprises."

I took a step, closing the distance between us, and saw emotion flare back into his eyes. This time, surprise.

"Leave me alone, Mark," I said, using his first name for the very first time. "Stop following me. I don't have anything to hide."

"Prove it," he said.

"How?"

"Take me to the prom."

"You have it backward," I said, my tone condescending and patient. "You're supposed to say, Claire, may *I* please take *you* to the prom."

"Not the Royer prom," Mark said impatiently. "The Beacon prom."

"I can't do that," I said, giving my head a toss to cover the fact that he'd totally caught me off guard. I really liked the way Claire's hair moved when I did that.

"I'm already going with Alex Crawford."

For just an instant, Mark's face became absolutely unreadable.

"I don't mean as a date," he said, his tone ever so slightly snide. "You'll need a staff photographer."

"Forget it," I said.

Without warning, he leaned down until our faces were close. *Omigod, he's going to kiss me,* I thought.

"Make me," he said. "You want me to back off, fine. Prove to me you're not Jo O'Connor and I'll do whatever you say. I'll flap my arms and fly to the moon."

"That won't be necessary," I said. "The other side of the room will be just fine."

He gave a breathy laugh, the air of it moving across my face, and eased back.

"So, do we have a deal or not?"

"What's so important about the prom?" I asked.

"Don't be stupid, Calloway," Mark said. "The ghost is practically expected. If she doesn't show, I'll know it's because you're not who you say you are. That Claire Calloway and the ghost of Jo O'Connor are one and the same. They can't be in the same place at the same time."

"That is the most ridiculous thing I've ever heard," I said, though my heart was beating so hard I thought for sure it was going to burst right through my clothes.

"Then you shouldn't have anything to worry about, should you?"

"I *don't* have anything to worry about," I said.

"Fine."

"Fine. I'll clear things with Rob. In the meantime, stay away from me, London. Or I might develop a sudden illness which will prevent me from attending the prom at all."

"Chicken," he said.

"You'd *so* like to think so."

This time when I attempted to move past him, he let me go. I'd only gone a few steps before he called after me.

"Hey, Calloway."

Reluctantly I turned back. "What?"

"Save me a dance, will you?"

I smiled sweetly. "Only if you wear one of those cute little plaid cummerbunds."

Twenty-three

The week before the prom passed slowly. Quietly. A thing I might have enjoyed if it hadn't felt quite so much like the lull before the tsunami. Mark kept his word—and kept his distance. He didn't offer me a ride once.

At Beacon, Jo O'Connor's last-minute nomination for prom queen had resulted in a last-minute location change for the prom itself. Rather than the usual hotel ball-room, prom would now be held in the campus gym. The consensus among the student body in general was that holding the event in surroundings with which she was familiar would make Jo's ghost more comfortable.

If she was comfortable, she was more likely to show.

In honor of the event, the decoration committee had gone fifties retro. It was a great idea, I had to admit. I might even have looked forward to attending, if I hadn't been quite so certain I was going to have an altogether miserable time.

I couldn't even consider the possibility of Jo's ghost appearing at the prom now that Mark London was attending, no matter how much I wanted to take him down a notch. I never should have let him goad me into helping him attend in the first place.

It was too late for regrets now.

By the time the Saturday of prom actually rolled around, I told myself I was resigned to my only course of action. Claire Calloway would attend the prom. The ghost of Jo O'Connor would not. Not even if she was elected prom queen. It wouldn't allay Mark's suspicions, but I told myself I could live with that.

Live with that. Ha ha. Very funny.

Prom would mark the end of my stint as a Beacon student. As of Friday afternoon, the journalism exchange would officially be over. Bright and early Monday morning, I'd return to being a full-time student at Royer. The whole Jo O'Connor ghost thing would simply die down. Things would go back to being as normal as they could be. Dad and I would continue to wait for the trial. With luck, it would be over by the time graduation rolled around so Dad could attend.

Life was going to be downright boring now that I thought about it. All I had to do was to make it through the prom.

Getting there in the first place required me to come as close as I'd ever come to telling my father an outright lie, an aspect of the situation I didn't care for much at all. Maybe that seems weird or goody-two-shoes to you.

Tough.

I love my father. He's been the only family I have for just about as long as I can remember, and we've always gotten along. His face lit up when I told him I was going to spend the evening hanging with a friend, and I struggled not to feel like a traitor.

"So this new school thing hasn't turned out so badly, I guess," my father commented.

I swallowed past the enormous lump that was suddenly filling my throat from side to side.

"It's okay," I answered. "The other kids are pretty nice."

"I'm glad to hear that, Jo-Jo."

"Any word yet on the trial?" I asked.

My father's face reassumed the serious expression I'd seen on it all too often in the last couple of weeks.

"Stan—Detective Mortensen—says he thinks next week. I won't be called right away, of course."

"Bet you'll be glad when it's all over."

"I will be," my father said softly. He gazed at nothing for a moment, a frown furrowing down between his eyebrows. "Jo."

"What?"

"Nothing," my father said. "Have a good time. Don't stay out too late."

"I will," I said. "And I won't."

I was rewarded when my father smiled. "How's midnight sound?" he asked.

"Peachy," I answered.

I longed for a pair of glass slippers all the way across town.

I wished for them even more when I stepped into the Beacon gym on prom night. It was like stepping into a fairy tale, of the somewhat fractured variety.

Enormous pieces of butcher paper completely covered the gym walls. On them, senior art students had created a combination of Sleeping Beauty's enchanted forest and a walk down memory lane. Blown up pictures of prom queens and kings from years past were surrounded by drawings of a garden decorated with enormous tissue paper flowers.

The white icicle lights you see·on every other house at Christmastime dangled down from the ceiling, interspersed with tiny brightly colored streamers made of shiny Mylar. Everywhere your eye turned, something twinkled or gleamed. A mirror ball hung down from the very center of the gym ceiling, ready to spin at a moment's notice.

Even the area reserved for the taking of the requisite souvenir photograph continued the theme. Students could pose in front of a rose-entwined bower. I recognized it as a piece of scenery from a school production of *A Midsummer Night's Dream*.

Those who wanted something a little more unusual could poke their faces through a life-sized cut out of a prom king and queen, or pull period costume pieces from a dress-up box. Plainly the prom committee had taken full advantage of the fact that Mr. Barnes was this year's faculty advisor, a position that also made him head chaperone.

It was a prom no student in attendance was going to forget, even if Jo O'Connor's ghost did turn out to be a no-show.

After much discussion, I'd gotten Alex and Elaine to agree to let me meet them at the gym after Alex picked Elaine up at her house. Much as Elaine and I had dreamed of getting ready for our senior prom together, we'd decided I simply couldn't risk trying to pull off my Claire Calloway masquerade in front of her mom.

Believe it or not, I ended up changing clothes in the fancy bathroom of a down-town department store. A thing which might have been incredibly depressing were it not for the fact that everyone who came into the bathroom while I was doing my final primp got so psyched about it. By the time I actually arrived at the gym, I was feeling pretty good. Okay, so it wasn't the prom I'd dreamed of. But, speaking as someone who was supposed to be dead and therefore unable to attend at all, let me just say it was a whole lot better than nothing.

"You look great, Claire," Alex said as soon as he saw me.

He bounced up from the table where he and Elaine were sitting. In the dimmed light of the gym I could see several clumps of tables and chairs arranged around the periphery of the dance floor. On a dais at one end the band made various tuning up sounds.

"Thanks," I said. "Okay if I leave my stuff here?"

"Sure," Elaine said. She gave me a slightly strained smile. Elaine's dress was this beautiful peach color that sort of made her glow all over. It had a tight bodice and a long, floaty skirt. Actually, she was the one who looked as if she ought to be wearing the pair of glass slippers.

"You look fabulous, Elaine," I said as I slid my dressy shoulder bag onto the back of the one of the chairs and the canvas tote with my street clothes under the table.

"Sorry about the bigness," I said as casually as I could. "Reporter stuff. I'm here to work, after all."

"I like your dress too," Elaine put in.

In keeping with Claire Calloway's sense of fashion, I'd gone for basic black. Of course. Form fitting with a handkerchief hem that swirled around my calves. Tiny black beads decorated it at random, catching the light as I walked.

I'd piled Claire's hair up on top of my head. It was held in place by clips decorated with tiny chips of this really cool stone called marcasite. Like the beads on the dress, they sparkled in the light.

I'd gone easy on the makeup. A little soft color on my lips. Some smoky eyeliner and shadow to bring out my eyes. That effort was somewhat wasted behind the glasses. But I was pretty pleased with my look as a whole. Simple and sophisticated.

That was Claire Calloway's choice for the prom. Actually I was kind of starting to like Claire's fashion sense. Maybe I'd keep some of it around when I went back to being Jo O'Connor.

"And then of course there's Alex," I said, determined to lighten things up. If things got much more tense between Alex and Elaine, they'd need therapy before graduation. "I'm impressed. You wore a tux."

Alex's grin flashed across his face. "I like to think of myself as a trendsetter," he said modestly.

I let my gaze wander obviously around the room as if taking in the attire of the other guys.

"It seems to be working," I commented. "I think I see one or two more."

Alex laughed, and Elaine shot me a grateful smile. The band finished tuning, announced themselves, then launched into their first number. The crowd around us gave a spontaneous whoop of excitement. From all sides of the gym, students streamed out onto the dance floor. A sudden look of confusion crossed Alex's face.

"You guys go for it," I said quickly. "I'm just going to take a minute to review my plan of attack for the evening."

"Oh, but . . . ," Alex stuttered.

"It's all right," Elaine said. "Really, you two can go."

"Absolutely not," I said firmly, doing my very best imitation of Elaine's mother speaking to her younger brother, Dennis. "It's *your* prom."

"Well, if you're sure," Alex said.

"Sure I'm sure. Though if you make me say one more thing like that, I'll make you sound really stupid when I do my write-up."

Alex pulled Elaine to her feet. Together they moved off onto the dance floor. I watched the crowd part, then flow back around them.

"That was an incredibly nice thing you just did," a voice said.

I turned, unsurprised to discover Mark London. When I hadn't spotted him upon arriving at the gym, I'd briefly allowed my hopes to rise. Maybe he'd been bluffing, to see what I'd do. Maybe he wouldn't show up after all. Naturally I should have known better. But somehow, I wasn't nearly as distressed to see him as I'd thought I might be.

"I can be nice," I replied lightly, "as somebody else once said, if I recall."

Mark smiled at the memory of our first car trip together, then sat down at the table beside me, scooting his chair next to mine so that we could both watch the dancers gyrating on the dance floor.

"Why do you think what I did is nice?" I asked after a moment.

"Because you made it easy for him," Mark said.

"Easy for him to do what?"

He looked at me as if I'd suddenly grown an extra head. "For somebody so smart, you're not very observant, Calloway. It's obvious he's totally in love with her."

I could feel the hair on the back of my neck stand straight up.

"You mean *she's* in love with *him*," I corrected. "That's the thing that's obvious."

"Okay," Mark said agreeably. "If you say so. But watch the way he looks at her. You'll see what I mean."

I leaned forward, my eyes on Alex. The band was playing a fast number. As I watched, he captured one of Elaine's hands, refusing to let go as they boogied in time to the music. He tugged her a little closer to him, ducking his head close to hers to say something. It reminded me of when they'd played Romeo and Juliet and he'd stolen Romeo's first kiss. The intent expression on his face was just the same.

Oh. My. God, I thought as I suddenly remembered the strange look that had crossed his face following our one and only kiss. That was the moment he'd realized the truth, I thought.

Not Jo, so new and different. But Elaine, whom he'd known forever. She was the one Alex really wanted. A thing he'd discovered not when he'd kissed her, but when our lips had met but hadn't sparked.

He's never going to tell her.

I have no idea where that thought came from, but the minute it popped into my head, I knew I was right. In the normal course of events, Alex would have found a way. But Jo O'Connor's sudden death had put things so far off course that there was no hope of them ever getting back to normal.

Alex knew he loved Elaine. Elaine knew that she loved Alex.

But the only person who knew the truth, the whole truth, and nothing but the truth was the person who stood between them, dead or alive: Josephine Claire Calloway O'Connor.

What am I going to do? I thought.

"You're awfully quiet," Mark observed.

"I was just wondering," I said. "Wondering if he'll ever tell her."

Mark cocked his head to one side, his eyes on Elaine and Alex. "I doubt it," he said after a moment. "Crawford strikes me as the true-blue type. Now that Jo O'Connor's dead . . ." He let his voice trail off.

"Pretty much what I was thinking," I said.

"Of course," Mark said promptly, "if he knew that Jo was still alive . . ."

"You never give up, do you?" I asked.

He gave me his devil's grin. "Nope. So whaddaya think, Calloway? Do I get that dance?"

"Let's see the cummerbund."

His expression blandly agreeable, Mark

stood up. I laughed before I could help myself.

Mark's cummerbund was black with hot pink polka dots.

"I believe I specified plaid," I said.

"Give me a break here, will you Calloway? I got the ugliest one I could find."

"You definitely did do that," I said. I looked up, meeting his eyes. "One dance," I said. "We're supposed to be working, you know."

"One dance," he agreed as the first dance ended and the crowd applauded.

He held out a hand. I took it and let him ease me out onto the dance floor. The band settled into its first slow number and Mark London pulled me slowly but surely into his arms.

Dancing with Mark was like nothing I'd ever experienced before. It's hard to explain. The best I can do is to say that it was sort of like holding a live wire in my arms.

I could feel his body pressed along the length of mine. Leaner, stronger than I had thought. Feel a current of energy connecting us together. Touching Alex had made me tingle. But I'd never felt anything like this before. All my senses heightened, as if I'd suddenly become some kind of superhero with extraspecial powers.

This is what was missing before with Alex, I thought. With Alex, I'd felt attracted. With Mark, I felt alive. I could feel where each and every one of his fingers held me to him, pressed along the length of my spine. Feel his breath against my neck, his head bent to my shoulder.

Then, without warning, he lifted his head. With one hand, he tilted my chin up. In the flickering sparkle of the mirror ball overhead, I could see myself reflected in his eyes.

Except it isn't me, I thought. Jo O'Connor might be dreaming suddenly astonished romantic dreams. But Mark London believed he was holding Claire Calloway in his arms.

He wanted to kiss me. Was going to kiss me. I could see the desire, the intent, plain as day even in the gym's dim light.

I can't let him do it, I thought. *It isn't fair. It isn't right.*

"Don't," I whispered. "Please, just don't."

At that moment, the music ended. Not looking at me, Mark released me and stepped back as we both joined in the applause.

Twenty-four

After that I really did start to feel like Cinderella at the ball. All around me, people were having fun. But there was simply no way I could settle down and enjoy myself. Instead, like the ticking of a clock, one phrase repeated over and over inside my head:

The end is coming. The end is coming.

Sooner or later, the results of the prom queen and king elections would be announced, and the packed-to-capacity gym would get the answer to the question burning in the mind of each and every student present.

If Jo O'Connor was elected, would her ghost show up to wear the crown?

As the minutes clicked closer to eleven o'clock, the hour the results were due to be announced, I could feel the level of anticipation rise. Even Mark seemed caught up in the overall excitement, but that could have just been because he was waiting to be proved right. Jo O'Connor's ghost and Claire Calloway couldn't be in the same place at the same time.

They couldn't. I knew they couldn't. It was crazy to even consider such a possibility, let alone try to make it happen. But the longer I watched Alex and Elaine together, the more certain I became.

The only way they'd ever find happiness was if Jo's ghost made things right.

"You can't go with me," I said.

"Give it up, Calloway," Mark responded. "It's ten forty-five. I'm sticking to you like glue for at least the next twenty minutes."

"Fine," I said. "I hope you find the girls' bathroom an edifying experience. I think I'll just let you explain your presence to the chaperones."

"Oh, for crying out loud," Mark said.

He studied me for a moment as if trying to read my mind and figure out if I was up to something. Which, of course, I was. "Okay, but I'm waiting for you right over there." He pointed to a vantage point which had the entrance to the bathroom in plain view.

"Suit yourself," I said. "Take a few pictures of people going in and out while you're at it. I'm sure no one will mind."

Mark rolled his eyes and pointed. "What about over there?" he asked. This spot was slightly better as far as I was concerned, a clump of tables not far from the band. The bathroom entrance would be partially obscured by the band platform.

"Fine," I said. "See you in a few." Purposefully I walked toward the girls' bathroom.

So far, so good, I thought. *Now what am I going to do?*

Two seconds later the answer literally came right at me in the form of Khandi Kayne. I'd never been so glad to see someone in my whole life, which, you may consider a true measure of my current desperation.

"Khandi," I said as I seized her by the

arm. "You look fabulous! I'm so glad I ran into you. Remember that picture we were talking about the other day?"

Not giving her a chance to get a word in edgewise, I turned and pointed to Mark, who was staring at me with what I was pretty sure were narrowed eyes. I smiled and waved. After a moment, Mark lifted a hand.

"See that guy who's waving?" I asked. "He's the photographer for the paper. Tell him I said I wanted some shots of you. Let's see—maybe over there."

I pointed again, this time to a particularly large display of the paper flowers that festooned the walls. In a location which would require Mark to turn his back on the bathroom entrance in order to take the shots I was asking for.

"Tell him I said to shoot, oh, half a dozen. I want to make sure I have lots to choose from when I run my article on you."

"Thanks, um . . . ," Khandi said.

I gave her my best smile. "Claire. Claire Calloway," I said. Then I released her arm, and aimed her straight at Mark.

★

Safe inside the girls' bathroom, I counted to twenty while I gave myself a quick once-over in the mirror. My face was flushed, my eyes enormous. Neither of which was terribly surprising. I was about to undertake either the most thoughtful or the most idiotic action of my entire life. Both, most likely.

I gave myself an extra ten count just for good measure, thankful that the bathroom was deserted for the moment so no one could observe my somewhat odd behavior, then eased my head out around the door. Much to my delight, Mark was being totally monopolized by Khandi, who appeared to be giving him instructions on how to get the best shots.

So far, so good, I thought. Phase One of Project True Love was now complete. For Phase Two, I had to have help in the form of Mr. Barnes.

I found him over by the souvenir photo area, folding one of the costume pieces he'd brought along and stowing it in what I couldn't help but think of as the dress-up box. That's what my dad and I had called the one I'd had when I was little.

"Excuse me," I said. "Mr. Barnes?"

He straightened slowly.

Now what? I thought. Essentially my plan called for me to reveal I wasn't dead, then beg him to help me pretend that I was. Which, now that I was actually trying to execute it, I had to admit left a lot to be desired, as far as plans go.

"I know we've met, but I'm not sure we've ever really been introduced," I faltered.

At this, a faint smile flitted across his features.

"That's all right," he said quietly. His eyes looked steadily into mine. "I know who you are."

My mouth dropped open. There was absolutely no mistaking what he meant. I shook my head, trying to snap my brain cells back into functioning order.

"Okay, I just have to ask this before I can move on," I said. "How?"

Mr. Barnes's smile got just a little wider. "I came back into the theater that first day," he explained. "I'd forgotten something. I didn't actually mean to eavesdrop, but then I saw Alex go down."

"So you heard it all," I said.

He nodded. "Pretty much. It wasn't what I'd call a complete explanation, of course, but it was enough for me to know who you really are. Now I have a question for you, if that's all right."

"Of course," I said.

"Do you know what you're doing, Jo?"

"Not a hundred percent," I admitted. "But I'm trying to make that right. Will you help me, Mr. Barnes?"

"What did you have in mind?" he asked.

Quickly I outlined what I wanted to do. "Just think of it as a farewell performance," I urged. "After tonight, both the ghost and Claire Calloway will be gone. But Alex and Elaine will still be here. They'll know they can be together."

Mr. Barnes shook his head. "You should definitely consider being a producer when you grow up. You think big, I'll give you that much."

"I'm just trying to do the right thing," I said. "Please, Mr. Barnes."

"Don't beg," he instructed. "It makes you sound like a whiner."

"Sorry," I said immediately. He smiled. I smiled right back.

"Okay," he said with a sigh. He turned back to the dress-up box and rummaged for a moment. "Take off those ridiculous glasses and put this on."

The band counted down to eleven o'clock, just the way people do on New Year's Eve, only this time the clocks were off by an hour. In the moments right before the countdown began, Mr. Barnes and I dashed around the outside of the gym, then came in through the side door closest to the band platform. Now I was crouched down below it, waiting for the announcement of the election results. Mr. Barnes was hurrying back to his preassigned location. He was going to operate the special equipment that would illuminate the lucky winner: the spotlight.

During the actual announcements, the mirror ball and the spotlight would be the primary sources of light in the gym. If Jo O'Connor's name was called, Mr. Barnes would sweep the light wildly around the room. Concealed in the long, dark cloak he'd pulled from the costume box, I'd use the cover of darkness and general confusion to climb up onto the band platform. There, I'd be "discovered" by the spotlight.

I'd make my farewell speech. Mr. Barnes would kill the light, and I'd make good my escape.

All in an evening's work for a ghost devoted to the cause of true love. Or so I hoped.

From my position crounched beneath the platform, I heard the winner of prom king announced. I probably don't have to tell you that it was Alex. As I heard his name announced, I almost swore that I could feel my heart swell with happiness for him.

You really deserve this, Alex, I thought. Just like he deserved to celebrate with the girl he really loved. In another few seconds, I might have the chance to make that happen.

"And now," the principal, Mr. Bird, said, "the moment I know many of you have been waiting for. We had a rather unusual nomination for prom queen this year. One that I think reflects very well on the sense of community within our student body."

I heard a rustle of paper as Mr. Bird opened the folded piece of paper on which the name of the winner was written. That's how quiet the gym was.

"I'm pleased to inform you," he said, "that this year's prom queen is Jo O'Connor."

What I am about to say now will make me sound unbelievably full of myself. But I have to tell the truth about what happened next. I promised you the truth way back on page one.

The crowd went wild.

Students screamed, jumped up and down, and hugged each other. The mirror ball began to revolve. I could see the spotlight beam, sweeping wildly. My heart was beating so loudly it almost drowned out the cheers of the crowd.

This was the moment of truth.

You asked for this, Josephine Claire, I thought.

Before I could lose my nerve, I scooted out from underneath the riser and boosted myself up onto the platform.

Twenty-five

In the dim light the gym was a sea of eddying forms. Each time the spotlight moved, students swung in that direction, as if anticipating that the light would reveal the thing they were all waiting for: the ghost of former classmate Jo O'Connor.

I pulled in a deep breath, wrapped the cloak more securely around me to make sure my dress was covered, then eased myself forward just as Mr. Barnes swung the light back toward the band platform.

"Look—there she is!" I heard a voice cry out.

The light swooped across the platform once, twice, then steadied on my form. In the crowd of students closest to the platform, one of the girls screamed and collapsed into her date's arms. I was pretty sure it was Khandi Kayne.

I held up a hand for silence. Miraculously it fell. Unbelievable as it may seem, my former fellow students appeared genuinely convinced they were in the presence of a ghost.

My ghost.

"Thank you," I said.

The crowd gave a collective sigh. Out of the corner of my eye, I saw Alex start forward. Mr. Bird laid a hand on his arm and he checked. With the light in my eyes, I couldn't distinguish faces in the crowd. I had no idea where Elaine was.

"Thank you for this incredible honor and for making my presence here possible," I said. "I can only stay a few minutes and I . . . I won't be coming back."

A strange moan went through the assembled students.

"As I'm sure you've realized by now, it's not exactly natural for me to be here," I said. "I appreciate everything you've done to honor me, all the memorials. But now you have to let me go. That's the way it works. The way it's supposed to be. What you've done means more to me than I can say. But now we all have to move on.

"Before I go, though, I have a request."

I could sense a ripple of movement from the crowd. Students toward the front surged forward as they were jostled from behind. As if everyone wanted to get as close to the ghost as possible.

"I can't wear the prom queen crown tonight. I can't take part in the traditional dance between the king and queen. It simply isn't possible. But I think your king deserves a partner; he deserves a queen to hold in his arms.

"So I hope you'll agree it's appropriate for me to name a successor. The girl I'd most like to see wear the crown you've given me tonight. The girl I'd most like to see in the arms of the guy you've selected as your prom king."

"Who is it, Jo?" a voice I couldn't identify yelled out.

"I was hoping you'd ask that," I said. A ripple of laughter passed through my former fellow students. "I'm talking about the best friend a girl could have: Elaine Golden."

A hush fell over the crowd. Then, in an excited jabber of sound and movement, I saw a form being urged forward. In the next moment Elaine was being pulled onto the opposite side of the stage from where I stood, to take her place beside Alex. To say she looked dazed would be the understatement of the year.

"Thank you," I said again. "Students of Beacon High, thank you for giving me a place when I didn't have one. Thank you for teaching me the meaning of friendship. Thank you for one of the most amazing experiences of my life. It's over now, but I won't ever forget you."

I raised a hand as if to wave good-bye. This was the signal Mr. Barnes and I had agreed on. The spotlight winked out, then came back up on Elaine and Alex. In the darkness surrounding me, I turned and swiftly made my way to the back of the platform. Crouching at the edge, I hopped down. I could feel the hem of my dress catch. I yanked it free.

And then I was running for the door.

I did it! I thought. Jo's ghost had finally put in a successful appearance. It looked as if the third time really was the charm.

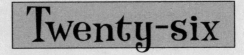

Twenty-six

Fast as my legs and high-heeled shoes could carry me, I dashed around to the front of the gym, whipping off the cloak as I ran along. It was from a previous year's production of *Dracula*, or so Mr. Barnes had informed me. Was that great or what? Now all I had to do was hope nobody was loitering near the entrance so that I could ditch the cloak, then blend in with the crowd.

My luck held. The only one standing near the entry to the prom as I panted up was Mr. Barnes. Silently he took the cloak from me and stowed it back in the costume chest.

"Nicely done."

"Thanks," I said, still a little out of breath. "I couldn't have done it without you."

"I'd like to hear the whole story someday," he said.

"You will. I promise."

"You'd better get back out there," he said.

"I will. Thanks again, Mr. Barnes."

Smoothing down my hair, I slipped back into the gym just as the band began to play a slow and dreamy song. The king and queen's traditional dance, I thought. I edged my way along the crowd.

Just grab your stuff and go, I told myself. I couldn't afford to hang around. Mark was bound to be looking for me, no doubt extremely annoyed because I'd managed to give him the slip and sic Khandi Kayne on him.

I located the table I'd shared briefly with Alex and Elaine, slid my shoulder bag off the back of the chair, then reached beneath the table for my canvas bag. My fingers closed around the handle. I dragged it out, then turned to go.

As I did so, my eyes fell on the dance

floor. There, surrounded by their fellow seniors, Alex and Elaine danced together, locked tight in each other's arms. If this had been a movie, instead of real life, this would have been one of those moments when you'd hear the music swell.

You know that saying about how people in love look radiant? I'd never known what it meant until now. But I swear that Alex and Elaine seemed to give off their own light. Their happiness was like a beacon you could see for miles. At the sight of them, my feet faltered. The truth was, I simply couldn't tear my eyes away.

"I have to admit, you're good, Calloway," a voice near my ear said. "Or should I say O'Connor? You had me wondering right up until the end, I'll say that much for you."

"I don't know what you mean," I said.

"Save it," said Mark London. He held up a hand. In it was a scrap of black fabric decorated with a smattering of shiny black beads that shimmered in the light.

My dress, I thought, suddenly remembering the moment when I'd caught it on something climbing down from the platform. Once I'd tugged free, I hadn't given it a second thought.

"I can't believe you had me so fooled," Mark went on, his voice bitter. "I actually thought that you were nice. Now I see you're just a heartless jerk. The only thing I don't know is why."

I took two steps forward and seized him by the shoulders. I could see his eyes widen in surprise. I spun him around toward Alex and Elaine.

"Look at them," I said, my voice an intense whisper. "Look at how happy they are, then tell me that I'm heartless."

"You're saying you did it all for them?" he asked. "That you did it all for love? How incredibly stupid do you think I am?"

All of a sudden I was completely exhausted. I'd done the best I could. I'd tried to make the people most important to me happy. Now Mark London was going to blow the whole thing sky high.

"Actually, I don't think you're stupid at all," I said as I stepped back and hefted my canvas bag up onto my shoulder. "Just misinformed."

"Then inform me," he said, blocking my way when I would have stepped around him. "Tell me why!"

"I can't do that," I said. "At least, not here and now. When I can explain, I promise you'll be the first in line."

"That's not good enough."

"I'm sincerely sorry to hear that," I said. "Right at this moment, it's the only offer I've got."

I moved toward the exit with Mark hot on my heels.

"How do you think people are going to feel when they find out you've deceived them?" he asked. "When they find out you've been playing them all for fools for weeks on end?"

I didn't answer until we were safely out in the parking lot. Then I turned to face him.

"Gee, I don't know, Mark. I imagine they'll be furious and hate me for it. Is that the point you're trying to make? I get it. Though, for the record, I never wanted to deceive anyone."

"Then why pretend to be dead in the first place?"

"I already told you I can't tell you."

"Then let me tell *you* something, Calloway—O'Connor—whatever your name is," Mark said in a furious voice. "I am going to write the tell-all article of your nightmares."

"Gee," I said. "Now there's a surprise."

I began to walk quickly through the parking lot in the direction of the street. If I didn't get away from him soon, I was going to do something completely disgusting, like disgrace myself and cry.

"Don't walk away from me. Where are you going?" Mark said.

"To the bus stop."

"What do you mean to the bus stop? Nobody leaves the prom on the bus."

"How the heck do you think I got here?" I all but shouted, rounding on him as a flood of frustration overcame my desire to cry. "In a carriage that will turn into a pumpkin at midnight?"

"Why didn't Crawford pick you up?"

"Because I wasn't his date," I said succinctly. "Elaine was. Is."

Mark dragged a hand through his hair. "My car's right over there," he said. "I'll drive you home."

"No way," I said. "And listen to you tell me what a lying jerk I am all the way across town? I think I'd rather walk."

Before I could take so much as a step back, Mark crossed the distance between us and yanked me into his arms. In the next moment, his mouth crashed down onto mine. Twice before I'd thought he was going to kiss me, but he hadn't. I guess he must have figured he had nothing to lose now.

The kiss was full of frustration, almost as full of frustration as of desire. It was a kiss that begged for mercy, took no prisoners, searched for answers, and made promises it could never keep, all at the same time.

In other words, it would have knocked my socks off if I'd been wearing any at the time. It certainly made my knees weak, a thing that probably would have annoyed the hell out of me if it hadn't been quite so exhilarating.

"That's the last thing I'm ever going to say to you," Mark said when the kiss was over.

In a silence that felt like a blackout at the end of the world, I let him drive me home.

Twenty-seven

The apartment was dark and quiet when I got home. I could see a band of light from beneath my father's door, hear the quiet murmur of his voice as he talked on the phone. *Must be Detective Mortensen,* I thought.

He was pretty much my father's only contact with the outside world, aside from me, of course. I hoped the fact that he and my dad were speaking so late at night didn't mean that something was wrong. Make that something else.

I went into my bedroom and undressed, hanging my ruined prom dress up in my closet. Then I took a quick shower, running the water almost too hot to stand. A shrink would no doubt relate that I was trying to punish myself. Then, pink as a lobster, I bundled myself into my jams and curled up beneath the equally pink chenille bedspread. I'd pretty much just pulled the covers up to my chin on my way to pulling them right over my head when I heard my father's door open. A moment later, he appeared in the open doorway to my room.

"Hey, Jo-Jo," he said.

I eased the covers back down to chest level. There was no sense in alarming my father by letting him see me with the covers over my head. Particularly since, somehow, I was going to have to find a way to confess all the things that had been happening the last few weeks to prepare him for the tell-all article Mark was no doubt composing at this very moment.

"How was your big night out?" my father asked.

"Okay," I said. I didn't sound all that convincing, even to my own ears. A shadow of a frown crossed my father's face. "Please notice the dutiful observation of curfew," I went on, determined to lighten the moment.

"Duly noted," my father said.

I pretty much expected him to turn and go back to his own room, but he hesitated in the doorway, as if uncertain whether to go forward or back. This was totally unlike him. If there was one thing my father was, it was decisive.

"You sure you're okay?" he finally asked.

"Sure I'm sure," I said. "Dad," I surprised myself by going on. "Can I ask you something?"

"Of course you can, Jo," my father said.

He moved into the room and sat down on the edge of my bed.

"Have you ever tried to do the right thing and totally had it blow up in your face?"

A strange expression moved across my father's face. "Maybe," he said.

I rolled my eyes. "I was sort of hoping for a yes or a no."

"Okay, well then let me ask you something," he said. "Do you think you had a miserable childhood?"

"What?" I asked.

"Your childhood, did it make you

unhappy?" my father asked. "I tried to do the right thing, moving us around all those years, but sometimes I wonder if I didn't get it all wrong instead. You never seemed to question the way we lived, so I thought you were happy, but . . ."

"I was happy, Dad," I said. "I didn't ask questions because it took me years to figure out that not everybody lived the way we did. Which may not make me all that bright, but it never made me unhappy."

My father gave a strangled laugh.

"There is one thing, though," I said.

"What's that?"

"There aren't any pictures of me. No record. It's sort of like I don't exist."

"What do you mean, no pictures?" my dad said.

"School pictures. Yearbooks. Things like that. I only realized it recently, but it makes me feel kind of weird."

Abruptly my dad stood up. "Be right back," he said.

I heard him move off down the hall. A moment later I heard the scrape of a dresser drawer being opened. Then my father returned carrying a large leather-bound object in his hands. He placed it in my lap, then sat down beside me on the bed.

"Try looking at this," he said

There was a word embossed on the book's front. Memories, it read. *It's a scrapbook,* I thought. One I had never seen before.

"Where did this come from?" I asked.

"It belonged to your grandmother," my father said. "Your mother's mother."

I sat up a little straighter. "You mean Old Mrs. Calloway, don't you? We were living in her house, weren't we? I mean, before all this happened."

My father nodded. "How did you know?" he asked.

"Something Elaine said. She told me we were living in Old Mrs. Calloway's house. I couldn't help but wonder. She kept a scrapbook about me?"

"Open it," my father said.

I did, and felt the tears rush to fill my eyes.

"It's you and Mom," I said.

The first few pages were all of my parents. Wedding pictures, followed by a whole series of my mom during which she grew progressively more pregnant. These culminated in a copy of my very first baby picture, taken in the hospital.

Josephine Claire, age 24 hours, a caption beneath the photo read.

For several more pages, the photographs continued to show me and either one or both of my parents. Then the photos of my mother stopped abruptly. The rest of the book was entirely comprised of photographs of me, carefully labeled according to year and place.

There I was in our living room in Bemidgi, in the apartment that, even at the age of ten, I'd known possessed the ugliest couch in the entire world. There was a picture of me in the kitchen when we'd lived in Vermont. I'd just finished decorating a batch of Christmas cookies. Proudly I held the tray out for inspection and photo documentation.

And then there were more recent ones from Oregon and Washington. My entire childhood contained within the pages of the scrapbook my grandmother had made. I wasn't a ghost. I had left a record. One created by the loving hands of the grandmother I had never met.

"I wish I'd known her," I whispered.

"We both wished that," my father said. "But we agreed that trying to get to me through your grandmother was one of the first things the killer might try. But I did my best to let her see her granddaughter growing up."

"I love you, Dad," I said.

My father reached out and tousled my hair, just like he always had. "I love you, too, sweetheart," he said.

We were silent for a moment, leafing through the scrapbook.

"What did Detective Mortensen want?" I asked.

"How did you know I was talking to Stan?" my father asked.

"Dad, please," I said. "Who else do you talk to?"

"The trial starts Monday," my father said.

My hands stilled on the scrapbook. "That's great, Dad," I said. "You can get the bad guy, then things can go back to normal, right?"

"That's the plan," Dad said. I heard him

suck in a breath. "There's something I have to tell you, Jo-Jo. Something I probably should have told you years ago, but I didn't know how. Who am I kidding? I still don't know how," my father said. "Something to do with my testimony at the trial."

Carefully I closed the scrapbook and set it aside. "What?" I asked.

My father scrubbed his hands across his face, just like he'd done the night I'd come home to discover we had to fake our own deaths.

"The murder I witnessed, the person who was killed. It was your mother, Jo."

Twenty-eight

"The killer's name is Orville Patterson," my father said.

"Wait a minute," I blurted out. "You're telling me mom was run over by some guy with the same name as the person who invented microwave popcorn? I'm not sure I can take this, Dad."

My father gave a surprised laugh. Then we just held onto one another for a moment, my head buried against his chest.

"Is his name really Orville?" I asked after a moment.

"It really is Orville," my father said. "Believe it or not, Orville Patterson was once a highly successful bank robber.

His nickname was the Chameleon."

"Don't tell me," I interrupted as I lifted my head. "He had a different disguise for every heist."

"Essentially that's correct," my father said. He scooted back until his back rested on the headboard, legs stretched out beside mine. "One of the things that made Patterson so successful was that, even with the aid of security cameras, law enforcement could only make an educated guess as to what he looked like. Nobody had actually seen his face."

"Is that why he . . ." I began, then found I couldn't go on. I simply wasn't ready to say out loud how my mother had actually died. That her death had been deliberate, not accidental. But my father was already answering my unspoken question.

"Part of what happened to your mother really *was* an accident," he said. "She was just plain in the wrong place at the wrong time. And because she was, she saw something she wasn't supposed to see."

"Omigod," I whispered. "The Chameleon. She saw what he really looked like."

My father nodded. "She did," he said.

"Some of the Chameleon's disguises were incredibly elaborate. This time he'd kept it simple: an oversized pair of sunglasses and a baseball cap. Apparently the cap was oversized too, because, as he came out of the bank, the wind blew it right off his head. When he didn't stop to pick it up, your mother retrieved it and ran after him. Naturally she had no idea who he was or what he'd just done. Neither of us did."

"Where were you?" I asked.

"Getting coffee," my father said. "I came out of the coffee shop, saw your mother retrieve the cap and hurry after this guy who was heading for the bank parking lot. I didn't really think anything of it. It was a small town, and she was friendly like that."

My dad closed his eyes for a fraction of a second, then opened them.

"He stopped to chat with her for a moment," he said. "To this day, I don't know why. Maybe he was getting some sort of cheap thrill out of the fact that she had no idea who she was talking to. He took the cap, tossed it in the backseat of his car. It was a big one, an old Lincoln.

"Your mom waved to me, then started

walking to the crosswalk on the corner. I remember he turned to see who she was waving to, then got into the car. He started the engine and pulled out into the street. Your mom was in the crosswalk by then.

"And that's when it happened," my dad said. "The alarms at the bank went off. People came pouring out of the building, and one of them yelled and pointed at the car. Patterson hit the gas. That big old Lincoln shot through that intersection like it was jet-propelled. Your mother never stood a chance. He hit her full on. I was maybe ten feet away from her, and there was nothing I could do. But the impact sent his sunglasses flying."

This time I was the one who closed my eyes. I could see the scene my father had described flickering like an old movie on the inside of my eyelids. See my mother hear the roar of the engine, turn her head toward the suddenly accelerating car.

What had she felt in those few moments? I wondered. Had she known she was about to die?

All of a sudden, my eyes flew open.

"The sunglasses," I blurted out. "You

saw his face. You have a photographic memory. You can identify him."

"That's right," my father said. "I've spent my entire life making sure Orville Patterson comes to justice. That your mother didn't die for nothing."

"*We've* spent our whole lives," I said as the true reason for his earlier worry that I'd had a miserable childhood became crystal clear. My father was afraid he'd sacrificed my happiness for the pursuit of my mother's killer. "I had a great childhood, Dad. I wouldn't change a second of it."

I threw my arms around him, giving him the biggest bear hug I could.

"I love you, Jo," my father said. "I seem to be saying that a lot tonight."

"It's not like it's a problem or anything," I said. We sat in silence for a moment. "Dad, would you do something for me?" I asked.

"Sure," my father said. "What did you have in mind?"

"Remember earlier when I sort of gave the impression I'd screwed something up? I think you can help me make it right," I said.

Twenty-nine

First thing Monday morning during journalism class at Royer, I walked right up to Mark London's desk. None of the other students seemed to be freaked to see me, a thing I had to figure meant he hadn't spilled the beans. Yet. Most likely he was saving it for the tell-all article.

"If you've come to beg, forget it," he said. He continued to perform the activity he'd been engaged in as I approached, jotting notes down on a yellow pad.

I slapped the morning edition of *The Seattle Times* down on top of it.

"There's a trial starting today you may want to follow."

He brushed the paper to one side and continued writing. "Oh really. And why would I want to do that?"

"Because it's kind of unusual," I said. "Specifically there are rumors of a surprise witness. One who could guarantee a conviction for the prosecution. The spokesperson for the defense is indicating his client isn't too worried as, just a few weeks ago, the witness was killed in a car crash."

Mark's hand stilled.

"What's the witness's name?" he asked.

"Chase William O'Connor," I said. "Sound familiar?"

Now, at last, Mark looked up, his dark eyes searching mine. "Let me make it easy for you," I said. "Chase William O'Connor is Jo O'Connor's dad. What would you say if I told you I could get an exclusive. An *exclusive* exclusive."

"I'd say I'd want to know the catch."

"There are two," I said. "One, you don't print your interview until after the trial is over. Two, you don't print *anything* about either O'Connor until you've interviewed Jo's dad. If you want to continue with the piece you're currently working on after hearing his story, that's up to you.

"Do we have a deal?"

"We have a deal," Mark said.

Justice from Beyond the Grave
Surprise Witness Shocks Defense

By Mark London,
Special to the *Seattle Times*

The defense in the trial of accused murderer Orville Patterson was shocked today by the appearance of a witness they believed would be unable to testify. Chase William O'Connor, husband of alleged victim Ellen Elizabeth O'Connor, appeared in court today and took the stand. This in spite of reports from several weeks ago indicating that O'Connor and his daughter, Josephine, had been killed in a fiery car crash.

"I did what was necessary to protect my family and see justice done," O'Connor said. "My only regret is that it's taken so long."

Nine years to be exact. That's

the amount of time it's taken for authorities to track down Patterson and bring him to trial. Both surviving O'Connors have indicated they will make further statements at the conclusion of the trial. . . .

The series of articles Mark wrote following his interviews with my father were something along the lines of a nine-day wonder. A thing which seemed only fitting, as it had taken nine years to convict my mother's killer. Not only that, there were nine articles.

In them, my father told his story. He talked about the decisions he'd made in the years between the two events that had so shaped his life: the death and the trial. And he talked about what he hoped the future might hold in store for both of us.

As soon as the trial was over and Patterson convicted, we moved back into Old Mrs. Calloway's house. I didn't return to Beacon, though. Instead I graduated from Royer with my dad and Detective Mortensen sitting side by side in the very front row. That made the paper too. As did the news of Detective Mortensen's promotion.

GHOST-GIRL GRADUATES. Is that a disgusting headline or what?

Mark did *not* write that particular article. Instead, he was so busy fielding sudden offers from colleges across the country, I hardly saw him at all.

Naturally, after my own was over, I thought about whether or not I should attend the Beacon graduation. Though Elaine informed me that most of my former classmates had forgiven me for my deception, the thrill of being even peripherally involved in a situation that felt like the plot for a movie of the week apparently being enough to cancel out any residual anger my actions may have caused, in the end, I decided not to go. I was still something of a celebrity. The Beacon graduation should be about its participants, not about me.

I settled for helping Elaine get dressed, and sending Alex a goofy card to which he did not reply. Instead, one day not long after graduation, he showed up at the house.

The doorbell rang on a rainy Saturday

afternoon. I was in my room. My father answered the door. He'd been doing that a lot lately. A couple of times I'd actually seen him go to the door when nobody was there and just open it and look out for a moment.

I think it was because he was finally free. No more captivity. No more running.

So when the doorbell sounded I hardly paid attention until my father knocked on my bedroom door.

"There's somebody here to see you, Jo," he said.

Alex was standing in the middle of the living room when I came out. Just for a minute, my heart stopped. Out of all the people who had the right to be absolutely furious with me, Alex had the very best cause. For weeks I'd been trying to think of the way to explain. To apologize. I still didn't know how.

"Hey, Alex," I said. *Omigod, we're right back where we started,* I thought. Me saying incredibly lame things while Alex just stands there.

Then he smiled. Not a strained smile, a genuine one. As if he was really, truly glad to see me.

"Hey, Jo."

My father bustled into the room. "I'm going for a walk," he announced.

"Dad, it's raining cats and dogs out there," I said.

"Really?" said my father. He leaned over one of the couches to peer out the window. "You're sure it's not just incredibly heavy fog?"

"You'll have to excuse him," I told Alex. "He hasn't been himself lately. The stress. You know."

"I understand," Alex answered solemnly, though I could see the laughter at the back of his blue eyes.

"Take your umbrella, Dad," I said.

"You know what?" my father answered. "I don't think so."

He left the house without another word, closing the front door gently behind him. In the silence that filled the living room, I could hear the rain tapping on the roof.

"Your dad is pretty great," Alex said.

"He is," I nodded. "The absolute best, in fact. Alex, I'm so sorry."

"No, don't, Jo," he said at once. "Don't

do that. That's why I came over. You don't owe me an apology."

"How can you possibly think that?" I asked.

Alex sat down on the nearest couch with a sigh. "I've been asking myself that question ever since I read the newspaper articles. I guess the truth is, I feel responsible for what happened too. I'm the one who declared I'd seen a ghost, after all."

"Tell me the truth," I said as I sat down beside him. "Did you *really* think you'd seen my ghost?"

"You know," Alex said, "for those first few seconds, I think I honestly did. I just couldn't come up with any other explanation for seeing you. I was so freaked, so confused, seeing a ghost didn't seem all that weird, somehow.

"I probably would have come to my senses sooner or later. Unfortunately I'd blurted it out in that counseling session in the meantime. After that the whole thing just sort of snowballed. I couldn't seem to get back in control no matter what I did."

"I'm familiar with the feeling," I sighed.

"Jo," Alex said. "You didn't stay away from Beacon because of me, did you?"

"No, Alex," I said swiftly. "Of course not. It just . . . seemed too much like going backward."

"Okay, I get that," Alex nodded.

There was silence. "How are things with Elaine?" I asked.

"Great," Alex said at once. "You know she's going to the U next year?"

I nodded. The "U" was the University of Washington.

"Well," Alex said. "So am I."

"What about Harvard?" I asked, surprised.

Alex shook his head. "That was always my dad's dream, never mine. I want . . . I don't know, simpler things, maybe. Different, anyhow. I want to stay in my hometown, go to the hometown college, play football. I'm sure I'll want to go away at some point. Just not right now."

All of a sudden he smiled. "I practiced my telling-dad-the-truth speech on Elaine till she could recite it from memory herself. It's a wonder we're still together."

"I'm glad, Alex," I said. "Glad you're going to get what you want."

"What about you?" he asked.

"I honestly don't know. But don't be surprised if you see me on campus. After all the moving around I've done, I'm thinking I'd like to stay put for a while."

"Maybe there's some dance we can all attend together," Alex said.

"Ooh. Low blow."

"Sorry," Alex said. "I had to get just one shot in."

"That's okay," I said. "You're probably entitled to more!"

"Pass," Alex said. He stood up. "Well, I guess I'd better go."

"Thanks for coming by. I really appreciate it," I said.

We walked to the door.

"See you around, Jo."

"Okay," I said. I reached for the doorknob just as the doorbell sounded for the second time that afternoon. "What is this?" I said. "Grand Central Station?"

I pulled the door open. Mark London was standing on the porch. At the sight of Alex, his face shuttered.

"Sorry," he said. "Bad timing."

"Nope," Alex said cheerfully. He stepped around me, then past Mark, and moved to the edge of the porch. "Try not to be stupid, London. If I hear you've hurt her, I may feel compelled to do something macho like break both your arms. I'm a jock. We can do things like that, you know."

Then he sauntered down the porch and out into the rain.

"So," Mark said after a moment. "You guys kiss and make up or something?"

"You are an idiot," I said. "You know perfectly well he and Elaine are crazy for each other. He's probably heading next door right now. If the only reason you're here is to be a pain, you'd better watch out because I'm planning to slam the door in your face."

"Don't," Mark said suddenly. "Don't make me go away, Jo."

I felt the breath back up in my lungs. "Just tell me what you want, London."

"To see you, for one thing," Mark said explosively. "You've been avoiding me for weeks."

"*I've* been avoiding *you*!" I all but shouted. "Who stopped talking to me as soon as his award-winning articles came out? What happened? You got what you wanted so you didn't need me anymore?"

"I can't believe you'd think that," Mark said.

"What am I supposed to think?" I said. "I don't even know you!"

"Stop," Mark said suddenly. "Just stop." With one quick motion he reached out and pulled me onto the porch and into his arms. "I didn't come to fight. God, you feel good."

"I am not a pushover," I mumbled against his chest. I felt, as well as heard, the rumble of his laughter.

"No, I know you're not."

He eased back, taking my face between his hands, running one thumb along my right cheekbone. "I know we don't know each other very well," he said. "That's going to change, beginning now. I want to spend as much time with you as possible."

"What about what I want?"

He kissed me then. Long and deep and slow. I felt my heart roll over inside my chest, then settle down to beat in time to his.

"What *do* you want?" Mark said when the kiss was over.

"I don't know," I confessed. If ever there was a moment for absolute truth, I figured now was the time. "Not altogether. But I'm pretty sure you're a part of it."

His lips twitched, with suppressed laughter or irritation, I couldn't quite tell.

"When do you think you'll know for sure?"

"Are we going to stand here and play twenty questions all day? How the heck should I know?"

He laughed then, the sound unlike anything I'd ever heard from him before. Open and joyous.

"I think I'm going to enjoy the next few months," he said.

I smiled. "Just so long as you don't mind a few surprises."

About the Author

Cameron Dokey did not play dead during her senior year, though some aspects of this story were inspired by real life. There really is a high school in Seattle with a fast food joint across the street, and in the parking lot of said fast food joint there used to be a car atop a column. Sadly, both have since been taken down. Not only that, the place no longer provides soft-serve ice cream, which is an incredibly big bummer. The name of the school is not Beacon, though it does begin with a B. There's no such place as Royer High. But a guy named Royer did used to be mayor of Seattle.

You get the idea.

Cameron's other titles for Simon & Schuster include *Beauty Sleep; The Storyteller's Daughter; Hindenburg, 1937; Avalanche 1910;* Buffy the Vampire Slayer: *Here Be Monsters;* Angel: *The Summoned;* and Charmed: *Truth and Consequences.*

侍

S
A
M
U
R
A
I

GIRL

侍

When I was six months old, I dropped from the sky—the lone survivor of a deadly Japanese plane crash. The newspapers named me Heaven. I was adopted by a wealthy family in Tokyo, pampered, and protected. For nineteen years, I thought I was lucky.

I'm learning how wrong I was.

I've lost the person I love most.
I've begun to uncover the truth about my family.
Now I'm being hunted. I must fight back, or die.
The old Heaven is gone.

I AM SAMURAI GIRL.

A new series from Simon Pulse

The Book of the Sword
The Book of the Shadow

BY CARRIE ASAI

Available in bookstores now

" *Once upon a time* . . . "